Winter's Crimes 22

WINTER'S CRIMES 22

edited by
HILARY HALE

MACMILLAN
LONDON

First published 1990 by
MACMILLAN LONDON LIMITED
4 Little Essex Street London WC2R 3LF
and Basingstoke

Associated companies in Auckland, Delhi, Dublin, Gaborone, Hamburg, Harare, Hong Kong, Johannesburg, Kuala Lumpur, Lagos, Manzini, Melbourne, Mexico City, Nairobi, New York, Singapore and Tokyo

ISBN 0-333-53733-5

A CIP catalogue record for this book is available from the British Library

Typeset by Macmillan Production Limited

Printed by Billing and Sons Limited, Worcester

Contents

Editor's Note vii

Living With Jimmy
by Robert Barnard 1

At Last, You Bitch
by Graham Ison 17

Shock Visit
by Peter Lovesey 29

Dinah, Reading
by John Malcolm 43

Pray Tell Me, Sir, Whose Dog Are You?
by Jennie Melville 63

Playback
by Ian Rankin 87

Murder *Ex* Africa
by Miles Tripp 111

Editor's Note

After last year's celebratory edition of *Winter's Crimes* the collection returns to a more familiar length. It also contains the familiar characteristics of presenting brand new short stories for the crime addicts who prefer their murder and mayhem in small bites.

It is always a pleasure and an honour to be the editor of such diverse criminal activities: a task which would be impossible without the outstanding qualities of the volume's contributors.

Hilary Hale

Living With Jimmy

by Robert Barnard

When I think about my mother in those years when I was growing up the image that comes into my mind is an ashtray – a large, shiny blue one, piled high – the neat brown filter tips nestling in the untidy rubble of grey ash. Eventually, when no more could be got into it, the ashtray would be tipped into the rubbish bin under the sink, but never washed. Then the process of filling it would begin over again. It stays in my mind, this ashtray, a still-life in blue, brown and grey – an image of my mother's boredom: I bored her, her life with me bored her, she bored herself. You can imagine how interesting my life was.

Meanness is unfortunately not one of my father's many faults. If he had been meaner then perhaps my mother would have been forced to get a job, find someone to mind me after school and in the holidays, see new people, perhaps even make friends. That way she might have met someone or done something interesting which we could have talked about when I came home from school. But as it was the alimony or maintenance money (she never said what it was, just calling it 'my money' when the cheque came in the post) arrived regularly, and was apparently generous. We never wanted for anything. And meanwhile my mother did a bit of cooking, a bit of housework, a bit of shopping, and went quietly mad with boredom, of which the filter tips in the ashtray were a symbol. I understand this very well now, at fifteen, but I think I understood it even then, though I would not have been able to find words for it. Naturally I worried more about the dismal quality of my own life.

About twice a year my father came to take me out. This enabled us to get to know each other better: he to find out that I was a thoroughly uninteresting little girl, I to find out that he was rather a nasty man. I, of course, hid my more interesting thoughts from him (one would hardly tell them to someone one saw twice a year), while he could not hide his essential qualities from me. The noise of his car starting up to drive him away always sounded in my ears like a sigh of relief.

Meanwhile on those days my mother had been loafing around the house, working up a good, acrid fug. She was never inventive enough to think up anything exciting to do while I was out of the way. She was what the tabloids would call an accident waiting to happen – or a bomb waiting to be exploded. Or a victim waiting to be murdered.

I was with her when she met Jimmy Wildman. It was holiday time, summer, so inevitably I was with her. There were clothes to buy for me for the start of the new school term, and my mother said she was tired of the 'filthy' local shops (she had a very limited vocabulary, which put me to shame on the rare occasions when she came to school functions). So we had driven in the little Allegro into Barstow, where we had found new shoes and a new coat for me, and done a bit of desultory shopping for her too. It was a hot day, and my mother had then declared that she felt like a drink – unusually for her, for drink was not one of her problems. We found a pub with would-be rustic wooden tables and benches outside, and my mother went into the bar and got an orange squash for me, and a gin and tonic for her.

Whether Jimmy Wildman sat down at the next table with a formed intention of picking her up I don't know. There were other, more desirable women there that morning, even if you were attracted by the smell of nicotine, and they were unencumbered with a child in attendance. I think I noticed him before my mother did, for I was sitting facing him and I noticed things because the bench was uncomfortable, like all benches.

He was wearing jeans and a loose denim jacket over an ill-fitting tee-shirt. He was big, but I thought it was the bigness of fat as much as of muscle (I was twelve then, you see, and beginning to notice young males and how they looked). His hands were rough, and a dark stubble sprouted on his chin and cheeks. His eyes were bloodshot, his skin white, his hair long and greasy. He was very unattractive.

My mother was rummaging in her handbag searching for a new packet of cigarettes and looking rather flushed.

'I'm getting hotter and hotter, not cooling down,' she muttered.

'Perhaps you shouldn't be drinking gin and tonic,' I said, looking round. 'Everyone else seems to be drinking beer and lager and stuff like that.'

She looked round.

'Do you know, I think you're right,' she said in a surprised voice, as if I had never said anything sensible in my life before. She pushed the half-finished drink away from her and marched back to the bar, cigarette hanging from her mouth.

It was that, the pushing away of the gin and tonic,

that told Jimmy Wildman that my mother had money. Not necessarily loads of money, but the sort of money that means you're not always worrying about money. Enough.

I saw it then, you see, as a matter of money. I can see now that there were other things. Sex, for example. Jimmy was recently out of jail, he was desperate for a woman, and if there were many more attractive women than my mother around, it was also true that they were women Jimmy was not likely to get to bed unless he took a lot of trouble with himself, which would certainly be unlike Jimmy. My mother, like her money, was enough.

'Got a light?'

He took no trouble, you notice, even with his opening gambit.

Within a couple of minutes he was at our table, drinking the remains of my mother's gin and tonic as if he were doing it a favour, and asking about the neighbourhood ('wondered whether it would be worth while slinging my hook here'). I don't remember much about the conversation, which was not memorable, only that before we left my mother said, 'There's a ladies' lav over there, Jennifer. Go and use it before we get in the car.'

'I don't want to go.'

'Do as I say. You'll only grizzle about wanting to go when we're on the road, you know you will.'

I had never in my life grizzled in the car about wanting to go to the lavatory. I knew then that we had not seen the last of Jimmy. I saw it for certain in the knowing manner with which they said goodbye.

He moved in two nights later. He arrived in the evening in a battered old car with one month to run of an MOT that must have been obtained sight-unseen. All his belongings, nothing much, were in the back of it. It was in the course of the evening that he told us he was just out of jail. He showed no embarrassment about it. When my mother asked what for he said with a shrug, 'Breaking and entering.' So unembarrassed was he that I thought he was telling the truth, though in fact he was not. He stayed the night as – shocked but fascinated – I had known he would.

I saw him next morning, on his way to the bathroom-lavatory, quite naked. It was the first time I had seen a grown man naked, and I can't say it interested me particularly. I was on my way downstairs, and I thought it would be impolite to take any particular notice. What I did notice, though, was that his sloppy clothes had misled me: there was a lot more muscle than fat. I should have guessed this. You do not get overfed in prison.

When I asked my mother she said that he'd be stopping for a bit.

'Do you know what you're doing?' I asked.

'I've been alone for so long,' she said, shrugging.

This was no grand passion, I concluded. But I said, 'I don't like it.'

'I'll see you don't come to any harm,' she said.

That possibility hadn't even occurred to me.

And so Jimmy Wildman settled down with us. His personal habits were far from nice. He ate hunched up over his plate, shovelling the food in in a hit and miss fashion. He spent much of the day in front of the television, watching cartoons for preference. His personal hygiene was appalling, but I never heard my mother try to do anything about this.

I began to think that Jimmy Wildman was not the sort of man a young girl ought to have around her in her impressionable years.

He used to go to pubs most evenings. Sometimes my mother would go with him; sometimes – if they were driving out somewhere, and there was little danger of my meeting anyone from school, or their parents, and being embarrassed – I would go too. On nice evenings we would sit outside the pub, and sometimes Jimmy would get quite jolly, and a group would gather around him, laughing. He would introduce himself to strangers by banging his chest and saying, 'Me Wild Man.'

I could have died, he was so common.

One of my father's reluctant and infrequent visits was promised for early October. One day on the stairs I happened to overhear my mother and Jimmy in the sitting-room.

'Jennifer's Dad's coming on Saturday. Best make yourself scarce.'

'Why the hell should I? Are you supposed to live like a bloody nun, when he upped and left you?'

'He's the goose that lays the golden eggs. We don't want him making any trouble about Jennifer.'

There was a pause and then Jimmy said, 'I'll take off for the day.'

I took that as a useful hint: the money coming in was for me, so it could be used to put pressure on my mother. On Saturday, when my father came to fetch me, he said he thought we'd go to the zoo. I made no objections, though I disapprove on principle of keeping animals in captivity. I thought it would be a good place to talk, so an hour or two later, when we were looking at a bored grizzly bear, and it was looking back at us boring each other, I said, 'Mummy's got a new boyfriend.'

'Has she now?'

I looked to see whether he was anticipating saving money, but my father has a very non-committal face, due to his not having very much in the way of interests or opinions.

'He's yucky. He's hulking and very working-class, and he's been in jail.'

'Well, I wouldn't want to say anything against your mother,' he said, preparing to, 'but she never had much taste, and she can hardly pick and choose at her time of life.'

Where, I wondered but did not say, did that leave him?

'He's got disgusting habits, and he doesn't even keep himself clean. He smells!'

'Hmmm.' (I could have been talking about the family dog.)

'It's not very nice for me, growing up with someone like that around.'

'No, it can't be. But I don't see what I can do. Your mother is a free agent.'

'There's the money you send her.'

'The money is for you. And it doesn't sound as if the boyfriend is in the high income bracket.'

Well, at least that confirmed my suspicion, but it didn't get me much further forward.

When he let me out of the car outside the semi I called home he said, 'Keep me posted about your mother's boyfriend.'

Thank you for your concern, I muttered to myself as I went through the gate and up the path to the door.

Jimmy kept away until late that evening. When he came back he was flushed with drink and was carrying a four-can pack of Export lager. I had noticed that my mother never seemed to give him any money for himself, but that after he'd been out in the evenings on his own he usually had cash to spare for the next day or two. I turned over in my mind what to make of this observation, but came to no conclusion. Since he always used the car – our car – I was unable to follow him to see what he was doing.

One day when I was talking to the headmistress about what I was to take next year I suddenly told her about him. It came out almost without my intending it.

'There's a man living in our house now. My mum's boyfriend. He's hulking and common – he just sits around all day eating and watching telly.'

'Oh dear,' said Miss Forster, interested.

'I think he could be violent.'

'Has there been any violence towards you or your mother?'

'Not towards me. I don't think there has yet against Mother, but I'm not sure. I'm afraid of him. He's not the sort of person who should be around a growing girl.'

'No, I can see that . . . But I'm not sure that there's anything I can do.'

She did, I later learned, ring my mother and make an appointment 'to talk over Jennifer's future'. My mother never turned up. Not that one could necessarily blame that on Jimmy. In the days before she met him she probably wouldn't have turned up for such a meeting either.

'I wish you'd get rid of Jimmy,' I said to my mother, a week or so after that. 'I don't like the way he keeps eyeing me. It's disgusting.'

'Eyeing you?'

'Yes – you know, sexually.'

'You don't know anything about it.'

'Yes, I do. I'm going to lock my door.'

'Go ahead. I know you're making it up because I know Jimmy doesn't fancy young girls. He fancies older women, thank God. I see who he eyes off when we're out together.'

She flounced out of the kitchen, bumping into the open door. She was very clumsy, my mother. I thought: well, that was another approach that didn't work. She was quite right. The women Jimmy looked at when we were out at pubs and places were all plump, maternal types. Pathetic I called it.

The next day the knock my mother had taken by bumping into the door had come up into a nasty blue bruise. I was pleased. I was standing at the bus-stop on my way to school when Mrs Horrocks from next door came past.

'Hello, Jennifer. How's your mother? I haven't seen her for ages.'

'She's all right . . . Well, not really. She's got this nasty bruise.'

'A bruise? How did she get that?'

'You know . . . That man . . . '

'Man? The one that's stopping with you?'

'Her boyfriend.'

'Well! I thought he was a cousin or nephew or something!'

I stared at the ground, and Mrs Horrocks went on her way, shaking her head. I congratulated myself that I had not even told her a lie, though I was quite willing to if necessary. I did later in the day when I went specially to see Miss Forster and tell her. She also shook her head.

'If only your mother had come to see me, dear. We could have talked it over. Perhaps *I* should go and pay a call on *her* . . . '

She did, later that day. My mother called her an interfering old bag when I got home that afternoon, and Miss Forster told me the next day that my mother had insisted that she collided with a door.

'Such a silly story. I'm beginning to be quite worried about you, dear.' She added, 'If you should ever need a home, Jenny dear, you can always rely on me.'

The next thing that happened was that the police came for Jimmy. They came on a Saturday when he was deeply absorbed in *The Flintstones* or *Corky the Cat*, and after a bit of talk in the living-room they took him away. I suppose he was 'helping the police with their enquiries', which I always thought was a very silly phrase: I couldn't see Jimmy as Dr Watson. My mother said, 'The bloody police. They always pick on past offenders.'

I shrugged and said, 'Seems a sensible place to start.' She got very ropey.

The annoying thing was that by late afternoon Jimmy was back and wanting to know what had happened to Corky the Cat. The police had hoped to pin a pilfering raid in Kettlesham on to him, but the night it had occurred he had been with my mother in Barstow, at the pub where they had met, and where they were by now fairly well known. Right man, wrong job. I conceived a low opinion of the local police which I have had no reason to alter since.

I need hardly say that the arrival of the policemen, and their going off with Jimmy, had been observed by the whole neighbourhood, most of them cleaning their cars or clearing up leaves on their front lawns at the time. I began to be showered with looks of pity when they passed me in the street.

It was now approaching Christmas. My mother had had no more accidents that showed, unfortunately: she was clumsy but not absolutely incapable physically. The thought of Christmas with Jimmy, and the endless diet of television pap aimed at people with a mental age of ten, was not pleasant. I said, 'I think we should go away for Christmas.'

It was typical of my mother that she had never thought of the idea of going away for Christmas for herself, and typical too that once it came up it appealed to her immensely: no fuss of cooking, decorating the house, stocking up with goodies. The burden reduced, in fact, to buying something for me (I always told her what I wanted), and this year something for Jimmy (almost anything in the clothes line would be acceptable, since his wardrobe was an Adidas bag). My mother said, uncertainly, 'But where do you *go*, if you go away for Christmas? What do people *do*?'

'They go to hotels. There's one in the paper tonight offering a three-day Christmas away-break, at Seccombe.'

'It would be *nice*.'

'A hundred and fifty pounds all in, children at half price.'

'I suppose I could manage that.'

'Jimmy would need some new clothes,' I pointed out.

'Oh, that's all right. I was thinking of kitting him out for Christmas anyway.'

Jimmy did not look particularly gratified or even interested, and he didn't say what he was thinking of getting her: it depended, presumably, on what he could pick up.

'I could ring them and book,' I said.

I have a very adult voice, and an excellent vocabulary. It was always best to do things like that myself, since if I left it to Mother it would probably not get done. After some thought I booked us in as Mr and Mrs Wildman and Jennifer Burton (child). Child of a previous marriage, I impressed on my mother.

'I don't know why I should lie about being married to Jimmy,' she complained. 'Nobody cares these days.'

'They would care at a hotel in Seccombe,' I said, and added nastily, 'It looks bad enough as it is.'

That, as it turned out, was putting it mildly. The clientèle at the Devonshire Arms at Seccombe were fiftyish or over, twin-set and pearls if they were women, tweeds and pipes if they were men. Middle-aged women with toy-boys were not part of their mental world. They gave the impression that they had spent their lives choking off unwanted familiarities, and it seemed as if the whole point for them of celebrating Christmas in a hotel was to show that they knew how to Keep Themselves to Themselves. Jimmy in a suit and tie only meant that the temperature was nine below instead of ten below. Any communication there was occurred between the men in the bars, where it was established that the 'marriage' of Jimmy and my mother was recent, and I was not his child. It was immediately assumed I was an illegitimate product of my mother's gay youth, and I was 'poor deared' by the kindlier of the women there, and pointedly ignored by the beastlier. Any attempts at jollity at our table (and Jimmy only tried two or three times) lowered the temperature in the room still further.

It didn't worry my mother. To care what other people think of you, you have first to notice. She ate the food, which was conventional but good, drank the odd glass of wine, leaving the rest of the bottle to Jimmy, and generally seemed to have quite a satisfactory time of it. They spent a lot of time in bed, but as there was television in each room they could well have been watching *The Sound of Music*.

I had announced from the beginning that I wanted to go to Hatherton Towers. That is the point about Seccombe. It is a very snooty little town, but the nearest stately home has been turned into an enormous leisure park and funfair – a sort of Disneyland without the class. If my mother had known anything about me at all she would have found it surprising that I should want to go anywhere as childish and vulgar as Hatherton Towers, but when I asked she just nodded. I needn't have bothered insisting, in fact: Jimmy was determined to go anyway. It was aimed at his mental age.

We went on Boxing Day. It had been closed in the run-up to Christmas and on The Day itself, but on Boxing Day families start shaking themselves out of their overfed torpor and getting out and about. Normal families, I mean. My mother swore about the steep admission charges, but the man at the ticket office explained that the price covered all the amusements and sideshows. 'The little girl will have a whale of a time,' he said. I shot him a glance that should have shrivelled him, but he'd already gone on to smarming over the next family.

Well, Hatherton Towers had all the forced jollity and unforced vulgarity that I had expected, but I made myself go on a few things, and Jimmy capered around like a five-year-old, and would have gone on everything if there'd been time. I bided my time for an hour or so, until I saw what I wanted, and when I saw it I bided my time until the crowd moved in another direction, and then I pointed.

'I want to go on that.'

That was a super-high slide, snaking its way down round a central tower.

'Great!' said Jimmy, rubbing his hands and dancing towards it.

'You go,' said my mother. 'There's no bloody lift. I'm not climbing that ladder.'

'Come on,' I said, pulling her. 'I'm not going up there with him on my own.'

Grumbling, cursing, she started up.

'Come *on,*' shouted Jimmy down to us. 'It's going to be a great slide down! You've no energy!'

'Too bloody right!' shouted my mother back. 'I'm thirty-eight. I grew out of this sort of lark when I was fifteen.'

The sound of their voices penetrated back to the

odd family on the ground. It was the best I could do. I'd given up hope of organising a public row. Their temperaments were too similar. The word sluggardly would describe it best.

Jimmy was already at the top when we reached it. There was a waist-high fence which offered adequate protection for children. Jimmy was rubbing his hands at the top of the chute. My mother looked over the railings. 'Christ Almighty,' she said (she was inclined to blaspheme). 'All this bloody way up just to go down again.'

A second later she was on the ground, spreadeagled out, with a crowd gathered round her. A second or two later Jimmy arrived at the bottom of the chute to find her already dead. I meditated whether to go down on the slide, which was obviously the quickest way, but it would have given the impression of heartlessness, so I began screaming instead.

I must say I never expected Jimmy to be accused of murder. I had underestimated forensic science. My mother had fallen plumb downwards on her face, and there were marks on her back that could only have been caused by a hefty shove. The police had assumed it was an accident, but once the report came through they had no hesitation in arresting him, and the case was so straightforward it was quite swiftly brought to trial. I gave evidence that they'd had a bit of an argument on the way up, and implied that this was par for the course. I said I'd seen nothing on the top platform because I'd been looking over the railings on the other side.

The defence, a pushy young man supplied on legal aid, went in all directions in his unconvincing attempt to save Jimmy. I was not in court of course, but I had all the gen passed on to me by my school-friends. (Miss

Forster tried to protect me by keeping the newspapers from me – I'd asked to go to her as soon as I knew my mother was dead – but of course in a school everything gets out.) First the defence tried to shake the forensic evidence, but the expert said there was no way it could have been an accident. Then they tried to argue that Jimmy had found an easy berth, and there was no way he was going to ruin it. The young man pointed out that he was a criminal of the most petty variety: he had had two periods of probation, one involving community work (unsatisfactorily performed), and one three-month jail sentence, all for shop-lifting and petty pilfering (so much for breaking and entering – Jimmy couldn't have summoned up the nerve to break and enter to save his life). Defence pointed out that he had never been involved in violence, and the police had to agree with this. The police, in fact, seemed quite to like Jimmy, but they pointed out that he was an immature individual, was involved in a long-term relationship for the first time, and had acted on the spur of the moment. That was why they were willing to reduce the charge to manslaughter.

Defence then turned, gingerly, to me. I was young, and resented my mother's new affair, and perhaps was afraid of her lover. Prosecuting council vigorously objected. If the emotions were felt at all, they would not have been a motive for murdering the mother, but for murdering the lover. (Did they really think I was such a dumb-cluck as to commit a murder for which I would be the most likely suspect?) The forensic expert was recalled and expressed the view that it was most unlikely that a girl of twelve would have the necessary strength to inflict the blow that had sent my mother over the parapet (so much for experts).

I must say I did wonder whether the police would

do tests on the slide – whether they would find out that Jimmy could not have pushed my mother over and then arrived at the bottom a second or two later. But then, people's memories are not reliable where time is concerned, particularly at moments of crisis. And as I said, the local police are not all that bright.

So Jimmy was found guilty of manslaughter and sentenced to nine years. With remission for good conduct (and I can't see him having the nerve for anything else) he should be out in three or four years. I sometimes worry about this, but after all by then I will be at university, and what could he do if he found out where I was beyond accuse me? I just don't see him having the energy.

On the whole living with Miss Forster has worked out very well. When my father comes on his twice-yearly visit his face has an expression of relief on it, that someone could be found to take me on and relieve him of the responsibility. Miss Forster fusses a lot, is much too protective, but after my childhood this makes a nice change. It's true that recently there have been signs of something else that I certainly don't like – trying to get too close to me, touching me unnecessarily, that sort of thing. There's a teacher at school who's taken a big interest in me since my mother's death. Her family is grown up, so I could go and live with her. I wouldn't have to go to extremes with Miss Forster – just a few allegations to the police or the social worker who visits now and then would do the trick. I wouldn't think of doing anything more drastic. It would be unfortunate if people began to associate me with violent death.

At Last, You Bitch

By Graham Ison

'You've come to arrest me, haven't you, Mr Hardwick?' said Frame. 'I suppose it was foolish of me to imagine that I could escape the law.' He ran a hand across his bald head. 'God Almighty!' he said, 'I learned enough about it as a youngster to know that you can run – sometimes for a long time – but that eventually . . . ' He let the sentence trail and sat down, drained rather than relaxed, staring at the dying embers of the log fire. 'Funnily enough,' he went on, 'it's often your own conscience that does for you in the end. You can no longer live with what you've done. You feel . . . ' He paused, wondering exactly how to phrase those feelings. 'It's some desire for expiation, I suppose. A need to tell someone, and ask forgiveness. Not a priest – that would be no good to me, an atheist. I sometimes wish I was a believer, certainly have done of late, so that I could blame someone and ask forgiveness.' He looked up, a tired expression on his face. 'You'll have to excuse me,' he said, 'I've started to repeat myself.'

'Anything you say will be given in evidence,' said Hardwick. It was a brusque and jarring intervention that conflicted harshly with the ambience of the warm and comfortable room. He glanced across at the Sergeant seated in an armchair, writing. Hardwick would have preferred to conduct this interview at the police station where the requisite recording equipment was available, but he had no intention of stopping Frame now. He hadn't expected this sudden capitulation, not after all the enquiries and the scientific examination that had finally brought him face-to-face with his principal suspect. And then, as so often happens, his principal suspect had caved in.

'Yes, of course.' Frame looked up, his face twisted into a macabre half-grin. 'She ruined my life, that woman.'

'I suppose so.'

'I'd come down from Oxford with a degree in law, a good degree, although I say it myself. I thought it better to do that first.'

'First? I'm sorry, I— '

'Yes, before National Service. That was a cross all young men had to bear in those days.' He stared briefly at Hardwick. 'You'd have been too young, wouldn't you?' he said, and then nodded, answering his own question. 'In a sense, I have to bear some of the blame for what happened. There were two or three like me. Fresh down from university and straight into the army. We really thought we were it. And after the free-and-easy environment of Oxford, the army came as a bit of a shock. We resented those ignorant regulars: the corporals and sergeants. The sweepings of London, Liverpool and Glasgow, too thick to get a job in civvy street. That's what we thought in our intellectually superior way. Looking back, of course, I realise that they were the sort of men who'd saved this country. The type of NCO who'd borne the brunt of the fighting – in both wars – and displayed tremendous leadership qualities, not only to their subordinates, but to their officers as well:

young idiots like me, very often. But we despised them at the time. Their senseless shouting and bullying, and all this talk of the Russian threat. Mind you, I suppose it was very real then, the Cold War.' Frame took out a packet of cigarettes and offered it to Hardwick. 'I knew I'd get a commission, of course . . .' He broke off to laugh. 'The confidence of youth. Went off to Barton Stacey – down near Andover – and went through those ridiculous tests, just like circus animals being put through their paces. We all tended to treat it with contempt. Well, some of us did. There were others who were blatantly ambitious. Would have done anything, bloody hypocrites. But the one thing we all wanted was that little woven pip on our shoulders . . . have people saluting us, and saying 'Yes, sir' and 'No, sir', and the chance to get back at those damned ignorant corporals. I wanted that too, but I was contemptuous of the officers who were doing the testing. Regulars again, you see. Hidebound with military tradition. We went through all this rigmarole of trying to get barrels across imaginary rivers with the aid of scaffolding poles and pieces of wood and bits of rope, and nonsense of that sort. And all the while this Captain stood there – in a Scottish regiment, he was: wore a kilt and a funny hat – with a sarcastic expression on his face, writing things down on a clipboard. I'm afraid I regarded it all as a bit of a joke. But I was so confident of my own abilities that I thought they wouldn't dare fail me. I was too brilliant, too well-educated for them to turn me down . . .'

Hardwick nodded. He wanted to tell Frame to get on with it, but he knew that to do so might break the spell.

'But I did fail,' said Frame in a downcast, matter-of-fact way. 'It was a hell of a disappointment, and

I tried to console myself by saying that it was a sort of backhanded compliment. A statement that I wasn't like them.' He shrugged. 'We got back to Aldershot on a Saturday afternoon, and straight away split up into two groups. The passes and the failures: the haves and the have-nots, you might say.' He laughed. It was a grating and humourless sound. 'Actually they didn't say you'd failed: "Not recommended for OCS training" is what they put on the bit of paper.'

'OCS?'

'Officer Cadet School,' said Frame. 'There was one at Mons Barracks in Aldershot – that's where I'd've gone – or Eaton Hall in Cheshire.' He paused. 'Country seat of the Dukes of Westminster, I think.' It was irrelevant and he shook his head. 'Anyway, I wasn't going, and that was that. The six of us who'd failed went out on the town. Crombie, Marshall, Smith, Webster, Lomax . . . and me. Determined to get pissed out of our brains. And we did. We started at the NAAFI Club, and then went on a monumental pub crawl. Somewhere along the line we picked up a few girls. I think it was at a dance at the NAAFI Club. They always had one on Saturday nights. Married families mostly; but with National Service, there were a lot of young, single men in Aldershot at that time, and the local scrubbers used to come from miles around. There were four girls with us when we started on a round of the pubs. D'you know,' he said, interrupting himself, 'that there were nearly a hundred pubs in Aldershot in those days?' He shook his head in amazement. 'But then we split up. Marshall took one of the girls home, and Smith and Webster did the same with the other two, until there was Crombie, Lomax and myself left. And Shirley West.' He said the name bitterly and stared into the fireplace. 'It was a glorious summer's night, and . . .'

For a moment he paused, staring at Hardwick. 'I seem to remember that we went to a fair at some stage, down near the gasworks. There is a gasworks in Aldershot, isn't there?' Hardwick shrugged. 'Yes,' continued Frame. 'We all went on the big dipper. I'd had so much to drink that when we got down again, I was sick. All that beer getting shaken up, I suppose. Crazy, the things you do when you're young. Anyhow, we finished up at the back of the hospital. Cambridge Military on Gun Hill. There used to be some secluded ground there, a small wood. It's probably been built on now; I've never been back, not to Gun Hill. We'd all had a skinful by then, Shirley included. And that's when it happened. And I had no part of it. It was Crombie who started it. He got Shirley up against a tree and started kissing her, pushing himself against her and trying to pull her skirt up. You know the sort of thing. Well she struggled a bit at first, and giggled a lot, and the way she struggled made it seem as though she was joking . . . at least that's what we thought. All a bit light-hearted, the way girls do. Saying "No" when they really mean "Yes". Anyway, Crombie got most of her clothes off and then got her down on the ground and screwed her. He actually screwed her with us watching.' Frame shook his head slowly, as if still unable to accept what he'd seen all those years ago. 'I can still remember seeing his bare arse going up and down, all white in the moonlight. She was still struggling, but we thought it was all good fun. I mean, she didn't scream, not real screams. She just kept saying "No" and "You mustn't" . . . things like that; the sort of things girls say when they mean the exact opposite. Well that's what we thought: thought she was willing but playing hard to get. But I didn't know. I'd never had a woman, you see. Not then. I was just a kid. Didn't know how women really reacted. Didn't know whether "stop" actually meant stop, or whether it meant don't stop. I still don't know, come to that. Anyway, it stirred me up, I can tell you, watching Crombie. Then suddenly he yelled out and just rolled off her and laid on the grass. She was completely naked by then, just laying there with her legs still apart, and whimpering. Then Lomax had a go. Christ, he was a bastard, that one. He was really violent with her, and she started screaming, really loud. Well that finished me. I suddenly realised that she wasn't willing and that what I'd just witnessed was rape. I knew all about that, having a law degree. It scared the bloody life out of me, I can tell you.'

'What did you do?' Hardwick had read the transcript of the trial, but Frame was telling a different story.

'I ran like hell, all the way back to barracks. It was late by then. We were supposed to be in by twenty-two fifteen – we were still in training, you see – but it was well past that. I must have been mad, but you don't think. If I'd shown up at the guardroom then, I'd have been put on a fizzer for being late and being drunk, but that would have been better than what happened.'

'And what did happen?'

'I went in over the wall and went to bed.'

'Over the wall?' Hardwick raised an eyebrow. There had been nothing about walls in the transcript.

'A figure of speech. There weren't any walls. They were the old Victorian barracks in those days; bloody awful, they were, but if you knew your way about, you could get to your barrack block without going anywhere near the guardroom. About half an hour later, Crombie and Lomax came in. They'd come over the wall, too, and got straight into bed. We were all very quiet. Afraid of waking up the Corporal whose bunk was in a separate room at the end, you see.'

'What time was it by then?' asked Hardwick.

'About midnight, I suppose. Anyway, at about two o'clock, all hell was let loose. The door flew open and the room was full of military police. And Crombie, Lomax and I were arrested. They were nasty bastards, the military police, but fortunately the civil police were with them, and they knew all about the dangers of roughing-up prisoners. We were told to get dressed in our denims— '

'Why denims?'

'They took our battledresses. That's what we'd been wearing when we went out. Wanted them for the forensic science lab, I suppose. In next to no time, we were all in Aldershot police station.'

'What happened then?'

'We were questioned, one at a time, by a detective inspector, about where we'd been and what we'd done.'

'And did you tell him what you've just told me?'

'Yes, of course I did, but he didn't believe me. He asked me why I hadn't gone straight to the police and reported what I'd seen, if that was the case. He said that if I'd got a degree in law, I should have known that a serious crime had been committed. Then he asked me why I hadn't booked in at the guardroom. I said I didn't know, and he said it was because I'd just committed rape and had come in with the other two. And because we'd all been so quiet coming in, so as not to wake the Corporal, there was no one in the barrack room who'd heard me come in first. Most times your mates would cover for you, even if they hadn't heard you, but once they knew what this was all about, they didn't want to know. Don't blame them really. Could have finished up being done for perjury or some such thing, I suppose. As it happened, it wouldn't have made any difference to Crombie and Lomax: they both admitted it, but said that Shirley had been willing, and that anyway they'd been too drunk to know what they were doing.'

'But the police didn't believe you?'

'No. I hadn't been as drunk as the other two. Once I'd been sick – after getting off the big dipper – I was almost sober again. I kept repeating that I hadn't raped her. I kept telling everyone, even at the trial.' Frame looked at Hardwick, challenging him to argue. 'But in the end I was so confused that I didn't know what I was saying. But then you wouldn't know what it's like to be interrogated by the police.' Frame looked at Hardwick, the trace of a sneer on his face.

'Don't you believe it,' said Hardwick, thinking back to the occasion when, as a detective sergeant, he had been involved in a rather nasty – and wholly unjustified – allegation of wounding a prisoner, and the brute force of a neighbouring police force had descended on his station and questioned him for three hours. 'Go on.'

'The next morning we were put on an identification parade – one at a time – and this Shirley West picked me out as one of the soldiers who'd raped her.'

'And that, I suppose, was that?'

Frame stared malevolently at Hardwick. 'That's one way of putting it. We were tried at Hampshire Assizes – at Winchester – and I got seven years for a rape I didn't commit. And you wonder why I'm bitter. They took the word of that little tart against mine.'

'Did you appeal?' asked Hardwick.

'Of course I appealed. Didn't do any good, though.'

'And afterwards? Didn't you take the case up with the Home Secretary?'

Frame scoffed. 'What would have been the point? Shirley West had stood in the witness box at Winchester and pointed me out as one of the soldiers who'd raped her. Me, Crombie and Lomax.'

'What about Crombie and Lomax? Didn't they say that you hadn't?'

Frame laughed savagely. 'They said they were too drunk to remember what had happened. That was part of their defence . . . or rather their plea in mitigation. They could hardly have said that they didn't remember raping Shirley West but did remember that I hadn't touched her. Anyway, to cut a long story short, young Miss West put paid to my becoming a solicitor. They don't admit convicted rapists to the Law Society. I had to get a job as a clerk. That was demeaning, knowing that I had a degree . . . better qualified than most people of my age at the time.' Whatever else he may have been guilty of, no one could ever accuse Frame of false modesty.

'But things obviously got better.'

'Oh yes, but no thanks to Shirley West. The fact that I'm now a success in business was due entirely to my own efforts . . . mine and my late wife's. I'd almost forgotten Shirley West . . . as much as one can forget in circumstances like those. Then one day I saw her. It was the most remarkable thing. It had been years since I'd last been in Aldershot. I'd stopped at traffic lights – at the top end of Queen's Avenue, beyond North Camp – and I glanced across at the other driver, the way one does. And there she was: Shirley West. It was thirty-five years since I'd seen her in the witness box at Winchester, but she hadn't changed. I knew it was her immediately. You don't forget someone who's done something like that to you.'

'What did you do?'

'Nothing. Not then. The lights changed and we

moved off, but I followed her. Found out where she lived.'

'Did you speak to her then?'

'No. There was no rush. After all, I'd waited thirty-five years, and I wanted to work out what I was going to say to her.'

'And that's when you decided to exact your revenge, was it?'

'No, not revenge. I just wanted to see her and get her to admit that she'd been wrong. It was too late for anything else; too late to think about becoming a solicitor now.' He broke off to laugh at the thought. 'It wasn't difficult to find out more about her. Now she was called Shirley Goodson, Mrs Shirley Goodson, and was married to a soldier. That was inevitable, I suppose. Then I heard that her husband's battalion had been posted to Northern Ireland. It's surprising what you can pick up in the pubs around Aldershot. I guessed that her husband would have left her here, so I went to see her one night.'

'What did you say to her?'

'I told her what she'd done to my life, and I tried to get her to admit that she'd been wrong, or that she'd been confused that night.'

'And did she? Admit it, I mean.' Hardwick knew the answer to that.

'No. She denied ever having seen me before. Well that was understandable. I've changed a lot. I lost most of my hair in prison, even though I was only a young man, but that was the trauma of it all, I suppose. But she said she'd never been involved in anything like that. Said she'd never been raped.'

'What did you say to that?'

'I'm afraid that I got rather angry: her not having the courage to admit it. As if it would have made any difference after all that time. I said that she was right . . . that she certainly hadn't been raped by me. She accused me of being mad, and threatened to call the police. And that's when things started to go wrong. I told her that although I'd been convicted of her rape all those years ago, I hadn't raped her. So I was going to rape her now. I wasn't serious. I just wanted to frighten her, make her see what a wreck she'd made of my life, but she thought I meant it.'

'I'm not surprised,' said Hardwick.

'It obviously frightened her, because she made a rush for the telephone. Well, I tried to stop her, naturally, and she attacked me. Like a wildcat, she was. Screaming and kicking just as she had been on the night when Lomax raped her. I was trying to defend myself, fighting her off. I realised that it had been a mistake, going there. I should have left it. Then she picked up this knife – an ornamental dagger it was: the sort of souvenir that service families bring back from places like Hong Kong – and came for me. I grabbed her wrist and turned it. It was then that she tripped forward, on to the blade. She must have been dead before she hit the floor.'

'And then you ran away. Again.' Hardwick's voice was hard. He didn't believe the last part of Frame's account, but he had good cause not to.

'Yes, I'm afraid so.'

'Well, be that as it may,' said Hardwick. 'I'm charging you with murder— '

'But it wasn't murder, it was an accident.' Frame spoke desperately, sitting forward, his hands linked between his knees. 'But I don't suppose anyone will believe it.'

'No, they won't,' said Hardwick, 'because we found the note.'

'What?' The look of shock on Frame's face was so obviously genuine that it was clear that he'd forgotten all about the note.

Hardwick withdrew a small plastic envelope from his inside pocket and laid it on the coffee table. 'This note.'

Frame leaned forward and stared at the words. Words that condemned him: AT LAST, YOU BITCH.

'But the real irony of it, Mr Frame, is that Mrs Goodson wasn't Shirley West. Mrs Goodson's maiden name was Purves, and she was born in Harrogate. Shirley West, who you claim falsely accused you of raping her, died in 1957 at the age of twenty-one.' Hardwick stood up and nodded to the Sergeant. 'She committed suicide,' he said.

Shock Visit

by Peter Lovesey

Just as Mrs Bloomfield was reaching for the phone a shaft of sunlight dazzled her. Out in the street someone had opened a car door. She had no idea whose car it was. It had drawn up plumb in front of the house.

A man in tinted glasses climbed out, stared straight at the house as if making up his mind and then dipped to remove a briefcase from the car's interior. Mrs Bloomfield let out a troubled breath. She had never seen the man before, but from the look of him he was from one of those religious sects that knocked on doors. They always wore dark suits and white shirts and carried cases containing their literature. And they invariably looked as if they hadn't eaten a good meal in weeks. They usually came in twos, however. She couldn't see a second man yet. She retreated to the far side of the living-room where she couldn't possibly be spotted from outside.

The click of the front gate was so long in coming that she was encouraged to hope that the man had decided to try another house further up the street. She inched forward, curiosity overcoming caution, and peered out. The same man was still out there on the other side of the privet hedge. He had his hands up to his face. Did they offer up prayers before they knocked? Mrs Bloomfield asked herself.

She said aloud on a note of despair. 'Oh, no – why me?' and backed away from the window.

Now the gate definitely clicked and steps came up the path. Mrs Bloomfield fingered the silver crucifix at her throat. She didn't propose to discuss her beliefs with anybody, let alone a stranger. She would not go to the door. Let him give up and go away, whatever he wanted.

The doorbell chimed its two disarming notes.

There was nothing to show she was at home. The car was in the garage with the door closed.

The chimes sounded again. And again, several times over.

The caller's persistence undermined Mrs Bloomfield's resolve a little. She had a safety chain on the door. She could always ask what he wanted and tell him to go away. That was the reasonable thing to do. First, she needed another look at him to make absolutely sure it was nobody she knew. If it turned out to be a friend who had come on an unexpected visit she couldn't very well slam the door in his face.

The curve of the bow window gave a narrow view of the porch. All she had to do was make a space between the edge of the curtain and the window frame.

She sidled closer and eased the curtain aside with a fingertip. The man wasn't at the door any longer. In her agitated state she had failed to notice that the chimes had stopped. Had he given up? She bit her lip and shut her eyes and willed him to get in his car and drive off. Her strength of will must have been less than his, for when she opened her eyes she was looking straight into his face. He was only a yard away from her, standing right up to the window, gesturing, jabbing his finger towards the door. Mrs Bloomfield rocked back in a paroxysm of alarm, her hand to her heart. She backed right against the wall, beside the piano, where she couldn't possibly be seen from outside.

It was a monstrous intrusion, staring in at someone's window like that. No one had any right. She tried to slow down her breathing and get control of her nerves. Outrageous behaviour. He must have been standing on the flower-bed to have got so near. Well, she simply had to wait for him to go away. They always give up in the end, however persistent they seem, she told herself, as if she were thoroughly accustomed to getting rid of unwanted callers. She had an inner voice that sometimes surprised her by coming to her rescue in moments of stress; a firm, decisive voice that quite overrode the weaker tendencies of her personality. It was telling her to dismiss the visitor from her thoughts. Unclenching her hands, she moved into the hall and stood in front of the thermometer hanging on the wall above her husband's collection of miniature ceramic houses. It was mounted on wood and shaped like a guitar, with the glass tube along the narrow part. She didn't actually study the temperature so much as the painted scene on the guitar, of whitewashed buildings with red roofs and wooden balconies. There were palms and poinsettias and a strip of green-blue sea.

Feeling more calm, she turned towards the kitchen. She would put on the kettle. Forget all about him. Make herself a cup of hot, sweet tea.

She pushed open the kitchen door and went rigid. The man was standing by the draining-board. He had come in by the back door.

'How are you, Mrs Bloomfield?'

The blood rushed from her head. She felt as if

her body wasn't her own. She heard herself say in a whisper, 'What on earth . . . ?'

He took a step towards her and extended his hand. He was bone-thin and as tall as the fridge-freezer. 'I came round the back when I guessed you were having trouble with the front door. Is it jammed? I expect you had the catch down. It's easily done.'

'Get out! You have no right!'

He grinned oddly – inanely, Mrs Bloomfield thought – making a jerky little movement with his head. 'At first I thought you were hard of hearing.'

'Who are you?' she managed to say.

He fished in his pocket and handed a visiting card to her. 'David Tolpuddle. This won't take long, madam, I assure you.'

Mrs Bloomfield possessed two pairs of glasses. She called them her doing glasses and her seeing glasses. Unfortunately she happened to be wearing her seeing glasses which were no good for seeing anything so small as a visiting card.

She dropped the card on the table. She had found her forceful voice. 'Kindly leave my house at once.'

David Tolpuddle said, 'But we have an appointment.'

'Oh, no, we do not.'

'Two p.m. on Tuesday. It *is* Tuesday.'

'I don't know anything about this.'

'Pardon me, you *are* Mrs Bloomfield?'

'Well, yes.' Despite her sense of outrage, she found herself responding to his deferential tone.

'So we have an appointment.'

'Not to my knowledge.'

'Then I dare say your husband arranged it.'

'My husband?'

'Is Mr Bloomfield at home today?'

This is a try-on, she thought. Somehow he has

chanced on our name, perhaps in the phone book, or one of those lists the credit card companies sell to people. 'You had better tell me what this is about.'

Tolpuddle spread his hands as if to show how reasonable his business was. 'The valuation.'

'It's transparently obvious that you have made a mistake.'

He shook his head. Then he took a step towards Mrs Bloomfield that made her sway back. 'I hope you haven't already come to terms with one of my competitors, Mrs Bloomfield. That wouldn't be very ethical, would it, before I had an opportunity to quote?'

She stood her ground and said, 'Will you leave my house this instant or do I have to call the police?'

That patently shook him. His face twitched again. 'There's no need for that. I'm here in a professional capacity.'

'Do you call this professional, frightening me out of my wits, forcing your way into my house by the back door?'

He reddened. 'I wouldn't describe it as forcing. The door was unlocked. I was out of order to let myself in, I admit. I can only say in my defence that in my line of business one becomes accustomed to letting oneself into other people's houses.'

She wondered for a moment if he was confessing to being a housebreaker. She had never pictured a burglar in a pinstripe suit, but the newspapers every day were full of peculiar things that wouldn't have happened thirty years ago. A burglar with a visiting card?

As if he read her mind, he picked up the card from where she had dropped it on the kitchen table and held it out to her. 'I'm a valuer. You see? David Tolpuddle, estate agent and valuer.'

'Estate agent?'

'And valuer. I stress the word valuer because that is my purpose in being here, to make the valuation. People don't always think kindly of estate agents. It's a much maligned profession, Mrs Bloomfield. Let's admit it, the way you just spoke the words lacked the respect automatically accorded to a solicitor, say, or a bank manager. But I would argue that I am serving the public in a responsible capacity, just the same.'

Mrs Bloomfield's mystification grew as her panic diminished. 'Who sent you here?'

He cleared his throat. 'I wasn't *sent*, madam, I engaged to come. I am the chairman.'

'I don't know you.'

'My name is on the boards. Surely you have noticed our boards? Thomas and Tolpuddle, Estate Agents and Valuers. Sold!' He snapped his fingers and made Mrs Bloomfield start. 'My partner Archie Thomas retired six years ago. The decisions are mine alone. You must have seen the boards all over town. Red lettering on a blue background. Very eye-catching. As to why I'm here, I presume you invited me to come, or your husband did. You must have spoken to Angela in the office, the black girl with the endearing smile.'

'I most certainly did not – and my husband didn't ask you to come, I'm sure of that.'

'Oh, but somebody did, emphatically. Yesterday afternoon. Angela wrote it on the card. Wait a minute. We can check.' He put his briefcase on the table, opened it, took out a camera, a calculator and a couple of instruments Mrs Bloomfield had never seen before and leafed through the documents underneath. 'Got it! *"Valuation, 38 Bandmaster Street, two p.m., Tuesday 30 September. Mr B. Bloomfield."* It was your husband who came to the office.'

Mrs Bloomfield shook her head. 'It's a mistake.' Then

she added, 'Basil didn't mention it to me.' Immediately the inner voice told her that she shouldn't have spoken, for what she had said had weakened her case. 'Well, whatever the explanation may be, this house is not for sale.'

'Not yet. I always say no obligation and no fee. And now with your permission I'll just walk around and form an impression, make a few measurements.'

'You will not!'

'I would offer to come back some other time . . . '

'You'd be wasting your time.'

' . . . but that won't be possible,' said Tolpuddle, articulating his words in a slow, unstoppable rhythm. 'I'm in competition with four other agents, Mrs Bloomfield. This is a cut-throat business. If I delay the inspection I've no guarantee that you won't place your property with one of my competitors. For all I know, your husband may have invited them all to make valuations. That's the common practice. So I'd be a prize chump if I let this slip through my fingers. Let me show you how painless it is. I'll begin here. Switch on my tape-recorder, like so – that's for Angela to work from. Thirty-eight Bandmaster Street, Angela. Superior detached residence within a few minutes' walk of the local shopping parade, schools and railway station. In the kitchen we have Wrighton kitchen units, stainless steel double sink with mixer tap, Vent-Axia extractor fan, ceramic hob, Zanussi electric cooker – is the cooker to be included, Mrs Bloomfield? It's advisable when they're built in like this.'

Mrs Bloomfield was shaking. She couldn't reply.

'It's marginal to the final valuation, anyway,' said Tolpuddle. 'More of a selling-point really. Ceramic hob with four burners, Potterton gas-fired boiler. Cork-O-Plast floor tiles. Recessed lighting. Five power points.

Double-glazed window and steel-framed door and I think we're ready to measure up.' He pressed a button on the recorder, pocketed it and picked another instrument off the table. 'This is a clever little gadget. Did you, by any chance, watch the Olympic Games on television? If so, you may have seen the long jump in progress.'

He isn't a housebreaker or an estate agent, Mrs Bloomfield thought. He's escaped from a mental home. She said, more indulgently, 'I think you'd better leave now, don't you?'

He continued as if he hadn't heard, 'The way they measure the jumps may have caught your attention. The International Olympic Committee don't use tape-measures these days and nor do Thomas and Tolpuddle. It's all done with a gadget like this. You take a sighting of the two points you are measuring and read it off. Seventeen foot six. Splendid size for a kitchen but it wouldn't win a gold medal at the Olympics.' Smiling, he bundled everything into his briefcase and marched into the hall.

Mrs Bloomfield called out, 'You're wasting your time. I spoke to my husband as recently as Sunday evening and he told me he would never agree to move from here. Never.'

Tolpuddle turned and gave her a look of extraordinary intensity, like a horse disturbed in its grazing. 'You talked about moving?'

'Yes, and he was adamant.'

'Nevertheless you did discuss it?'

'Yes, but that doesn't mean— '

He stepped closer. 'How about you, Mrs Bloomfield? What are your wishes on the matter? Do I detect that you would like to move away from here?'

'That isn't the point.'

Tolpuddle smiled. 'Pardon me. It *is* the point. It is precisely the point. Where did you tell Mr Bloomfield you would like to live – somewhere abroad? Somewhere in the sun?' His eyes lighted on the souvenir thermometer. 'Tenerife. Am I right?'

She said as dismissively as she was able, 'It doesn't arise.'

'Doesn't it?' said Tolpuddle, holding a finger in the air. 'I wouldn't be quite so dogmatic if I were you. Tenerife. I don't blame you for thinking of Tenerife. Plenty of people retire to Tenerife. That's a very shrewd move with the market as it is. You'll get an extremely well-appointed villa over there for the price a superior property like this will fetch. As a matter of fact, one of the agencies I deal with recently sent me details of a particularly fine development in Tenerife. Los Gigantes. Do you know it? Handsome two-bedroom villas with a marvellous view across the water to the most spectacular cliffs. Perhaps your husband inspected the brochure when he called at the office yesterday. If he didn't, I'll send you one. No obligation.'

'He would have told me,' insisted Mrs Bloomfield.

'He must have wanted to surprise you. Pretended he wouldn't leave in a thousand years and then came straight to our office to arrange the valuation. What a charming surprise for you! We men may have tough exteriors, but underneath we're soft, as soft as you are, softer even.'

She remained unconvinced. 'When Basil's mind is made up, there's no shaking him. If you really want to know, he reduced me to tears – that's how charming it was. This is all a mistake – or someone is playing a dreadfully cruel joke on me.'

'No shaking him, you say, but you're speaking of

workaday matters,' said Tolpuddle. 'This was something else: one of the great decisions of your lives. How will the Bloomfields spend their retirement? Battling against the English climate for the rest of their days or basking in unending sunshine in the Canaries? I'm not surprised your Basil had second thoughts. But this isn't getting the valuation completed. Shall we look at the reception room?'

'No.'

Tolpuddle brushed the objection aside. 'I know exactly what you're going to say – you haven't had a chance to tidy up. I understand, Mrs Bloomfield. But *you* must understand that it doesn't make a jot of difference to me. I'm oblivious to ashtrays and newspapers. The state of your house is a matter of supreme indifference to me. No, that's badly phrased. Let me put it another way. I'm so impressed by its structural features and the state of repair, which is immaculate so far as I can see, that I have no eyes for the little things that make it a home. However, if you want to tidy up the reception room I'll take a look upstairs first.'

Mrs Bloomfield said, 'I'm going to call the police.'

She hadn't said it with conviction. The announcement was no deterrent to her visitor. He was already mounting the stairs. Halfway up, he leaned over the banisters and said, 'There's no need to come up unless you wish. Three bedrooms, is it, and the bathroom and separate w.c.? I won't take long. And if the bed isn't made yet, don't trouble yourself in the least.'

She didn't follow him upstairs. Neither did she call the police. She remained downstairs in the kitchen, unhappy and confused. It was unthinkable after that bitter argument on Sunday that Basil had changed his mind. He had never been one to relent. Anyway, he would have mentioned it. Surely he would have mentioned it yesterday or this morning, knowing that Mr Tolpuddle would call?

Faintly, she heard the movement of the footsteps upstairs and Tolpuddle's voice speaking into his tape-recorder as he passed from bedroom to bedroom. She went back to the kitchen and poured herself a brandy from the bottle she kept for emergencies. She was less concerned about Tolpuddle than she had been when he arrived.

He talked animatedly as he came downstairs. 'Immaculate, Mrs Bloomfield. We'll have no trouble finding a purchaser, assuming, of course, that you and your husband place the property in our hands. And you'll find that my commission is very competitive. I just need to look at the reception room – a through room, I believe I noticed from the outside when I was taking photographs. Very much in demand just now.'

'You took photographs?' She recalled seeing him with his hands to his face when she had assumed he had been saying prayers.

He was so far on with his sales patter that he seemed not to be listening any more. 'As a matter of fact I have a young couple on my books who are desperate to find a house like yours. Quite desperate. Wedding coming up in two months. And what is more, they have cash in hand. Do you know what that means, Mrs Bloomfield? No chain. He'll pay the asking price in good old Bank of England notes if you wish, and you can exchange contracts within a matter of days. Don't ask me how he got the money, but it's got a copper-bottom guarantee. I practise absolute discretion with my clients, buyers and vendors alike. Everything is treated in the strictest confidence. I could tell some secrets about the people in this town, but my lips are sealed.'

All of this made no impression on Mrs Bloomfield. She was trying to account for Basil's erratic behaviour. The invasion by Mr Tolpuddle had paled into insignificance.

Perhaps her preoccupations were transmitted in some way to Tolpuddle, because he suddenly said, 'Do you know what I think? It's love, that's what it is. True love.'

She snapped out of her reverie. 'What?'

'Love, Mrs Bloomfield. An act of love as beautiful as a poem. After the difference of opinion you had on Sunday your husband thought the matter over and saw how much it meant to you to retire to the Canaries. He's a proud man, not easily swayed once his mind is made up, but this decision came from the heart. He decided to put your happiness before his pride and he came to my office and arranged the valuation. He couldn't have signalled more clearly to you that he's ready to change his mind.' Tolpuddle beamed.

Mrs Bloomfield fingered her wedding ring, turning it on her finger. 'I can't believe a word of what you're saying.'

'Ah, but you must. You can't ignore a beautiful gesture like this. Accept it for what it is. When he comes in, tell him that you'd like to put your house on the market as soon as possible.'

That other voice of hers said acidly, 'You don't give up easily, do you?'

'Certainly not, my dear, because I'm pinning my confidence on you now. You and I are not really at cross-purposes at all. Our interests coincide.' He flushed at the good sense of what he had said. 'I'll finish the inspection now and you can have my valuation before I go.' He opened the door of what Mrs Bloomfield called her living-room and marched in, saying into the tape recorder, 'The reception room, Angela. Attractive through room with bow window and glazed patio door to paved terrace. Natural stone hearth with gas fire. Two double radiators. Telephone point.'

Mrs Bloomfield stood in the hall staring at the souvenir thermometer from Tenerife.

Tolpuddle didn't spend long in the living-room. In fact he stopped dictating rather abruptly. Mrs Bloomfield was in the kitchen when he emerged. She said, 'Are you satisfied now?'

He opened his mouth as if to speak and nothing came out.

Mrs Bloomfield swirled the brandy in her glass and swallowed the contents at a gulp. Then she told Tolpuddle, 'You shouldn't have forced your way in as you did.'

'You weren't locked at the back,' he pointed out.

'People usually come to the front door.'

'People usually answer the doorbell.'

'That doesn't excuse it, Mr Tolpuddle.' She took the glass to the sink and ran some water over it. 'Are you still certain that my husband called at your office yesterday afternoon?'

He looked shocked. 'It's on record. I showed you.'

'With a view to selling this house?'

'I assume so.'

She stared out of the window at the apples on the trees. 'He ought to have told me. Don't you think he ought to have told me?'

'I can't comment. That's personal, Mrs Bloomfield.'

'Just now you were commenting freely enough, telling me it was love that made him do it.'

'I suppose I got carried away.'

She sensed that he would leave soon. He needed an exit-line, that was all.

He wound himself up. 'My usual practice is to give an on-the-spot valuation and write to you later to confirm it.'

'I keep telling you I'm not interested. Isn't that clear to you by now?'

'Even so.'

'Goodbye, Mr Tolpuddle.'

'I'll get it in the post tonight. Just in case.'

He seemed to want to keep this fiction going to the very end. She sighed. 'If you wish.'

He fastened his briefcase. 'I won't press you for a decision. You have my card.'

'Yes.'

'One other thing. If you don't want any more agents to bother you, I should lock up at the back.'

Mrs Bloomfield rolled her eyes upwards. She had never met anyone so persistent. When she had closed the front door she walked into the living-room and watched him get into his car and drive away. The car fairly raced up the street.

She turned from the window, picked up the phone and dialled a number. 'Is that the police? I think you had better come and see me. I was going to call you an hour ago, but somebody called.'

They asked for her name and address.

While she was speaking she let her gaze travel slowly around the room, over the furniture she had dusted and polished for years, the table, chairs, piano, sideboard and china cabinet. This was her home, her address, and how she hated the place! Finally she allowed herself to look down at the carpet, at Basil's body, and beside it the candlestick she had used an hour ago to batter him to death.

Dinah, Reading

by John Malcolm

At breakfast on Saturday morning Sue expressed a hope that I could keep out of trouble while she was away visiting her mother in Bath. I grunted some reply or another whilst I looked at the auction catalogues and price lists that had come in the morning post. She was only going to be away for one night and it seemed unnecessary to respond to that sort of provocation; I perused the illustrations patiently while she got herself ready and then took her to Paddington in a taxi to catch the mid-morning train. Men are seldom as innocently employed as when among books so, as I walked back along Praed Street, I popped into Mr Goodston's shop to look for a read I'd promised myself. It started just as simply as that.

Mr Goodston was sitting behind his desk studying racing form. Sporting papers were propped up on the teetering stacks of books in front of him. Around the dingy shop ranks of subfusc bindings darkened the dusty air. I don't know why I like Mr Goodston, who is a cautious, fat man of great professionalism, but I suspect that it is because he flatters me with help and encouragement in a way that suggests that the younger generation are not prominent among his clients. In my work for the Art Investment Fund of

White's Bank I have had to do much research, not just of an art-historical nature, and Mr Goodston is both a well of information and a rich source of background anecdote. At home and in my office are the catalogues that trace the auction sale prices and the commercial movement of art; here lay countless volumes of memoir and social record that put life into the tableaux we purchase on behalf of our investors.

'Mr Simpson!' His eyes rolled up above the level of his half-moons. 'This is indeed an honour and a pleasure. The only rugby blue amongst my clientèle. I have admirals, generals and masters of foxhounds in plenty but of rugby men, alas, only one: yourself.' He smiled a trifle sadly and moved his papers to one side. Mr Goodston did not convey his usual bright impression and I suspected the papers in front of him. Mr Goodston has a weakness for the horses which consumes his literary profits. He is a punter. If his shop is closed you know that he is either in a nearby betting shop or on his way to one of the classic meetings. He cannot help it; Mr Goodston is a racing man.

'To what do I owe the pleasure?' He peered at me expectantly. 'Is it the stage again? Ellen Terry? Or a more sporting affair? Lily Langtry and Mr Moreton Frewen perhaps?' He put his finger up waggishly to tap the side of his nose.

'Not this time, Mr Goodston.'

'Aha! The plot thickens. Well, you know me, my dear sir.' He waved an expansive arm. 'Sporting, Military and Thespian specialities. Under what heading can I be of assist, as they say?'

'Naval, I think, Mr Goodston.'

'Naval? Naval! There you touch upon a chord, my dear young man. You touch a chord! Naval matters are dear to my heart. But not after the invention of steam. The Royal Navy was never quite the same after the invention of steam. I am purely a sailing man.'

'This would be eighteenth century, Mr Goodston. I was walking down the Portobello Road the other day, debating a holiday in Cartagena with Sue. The Portobello Road, as I'm sure you know, was named after a farm in that area which, in turn, was named, like the Scottish town, after— '

'Vernon's victory! My dear Mr Simpson! Old Grog! The hero of Porto Bello! Bells were rung up and down the country. Countless inns were renamed the Admiral Vernon. But a holiday in Cartagena? In Colombia? Is that not a fearsome prospect? Is that not dangerous?'

'Good gracious no, Mr Goodston. Colombia isn't all cocaine barons blazing machine-guns down the main streets. Cartagena is a wonderful example, a unique example of Spanish Colonial South America. It is a must on any professional tourist's list. Superb. I've always wanted to go there and see where Vernon failed. Never had the chance. Actually, it would probably be more dangerous to go to Porto Bello just now. You'd have to fly to Panama, nip up to Colon and then go by road out along the coast, with a pretty fair chance of being mugged or robbed along the way. I wouldn't mind seeing it, though. Beautiful harbour, I believe. The old forts are still there.'

Mr Goodston gazed at me fondly. 'Porto Bello,' he murmured. 'Vernon. Around 1739? Very exaggerated at the time, but the nation needed a victory over the Spanish. War of Jenkins' Ear. It wasn't that great a capture, really. Morgan had taken Porto Bello with his pirates sixty years earlier, but Morgan was a filthy rascal. Welsh. As cruel as Satan. The rich ladies of Porto Bello were strapped naked to red-hot baking ovens and roasted until they gave up their valuables. Filthy beast. Did worse things at Panama.'

I blinked. The dusty antiquarian bookshop of Mr Goodston in Praed Street is an odd place in which to conjure up visions of plump, rich, naked ladies being baked on stoves by roaring pirates but the imaginative mind needs no geographical movement for its stimulation. Bookshops exist for that reason. I cleared my throat.

'Is there a book on Vernon I could get hold of? There isn't one in print 'cos I've tried. I'd like to read about him and the great failure at Cartagena before I go there.'

Mr Goodston gave me a triumphant stare. 'Of course there is. And let me say that you have come to the right place because, by an extraordinary coincidence, I got a copy in a consignment of books, very valuable books, that came in after cataloguing this very morning. Look not so alarmed, dear boy. The Vernon book is not itself valuable. I had to take the er, chaff with the wheat, you might say. It can be had for a modest sum. *The Angry Admiral* by Cyril Hughes Hartmann. Heinemann, 1953. Vernon was not really so bad-tempered, you know, and his dispositions saved the country from invasion by the French in 1745, but Anson took the credit. Poor old Grog.' He hauled himself to his feet. 'The books are upstairs. Let me show you.'

I felt flattered. Mr Goodston had never before taken me up to his inner sanctum. I followed him obediently as he squeezed through a door at the back of the shop and we creaked up a staircase to the first floor. He fumbled with a key and we went into another book-lined room. Tea chests on the floor were full of books; Mr Goodston rummaged among them and emerged, triumphant, holding a red cloth volume.

'The very item! *The Angry Admiral*. I – is something the matter?'

He peered at me reproachfully, my attention having been diverted. His gaze followed mine to a painting hanging on the wall. It depicted a girl of perhaps eight or nine years old sitting at a kitchen table. She looked wistfully out of the canvas over a bowl of cereal.

'That's a Dod Proctor,' I said. 'I didn't know you had a Dod Proctor.'

A fond smile appeared on his lips. 'That is indeed a Dod Proctor. My late wife bought it many years ago. It is an odd item because there is a portrait of her husband Ernest on the back. I imagine it came from her studio – a sort of working canvas used on both sides. I am very fond of it. My goodness. I had no idea that your stewardship of White's Art Fund took your artistic interests so wide.'

I smiled back at him. 'White's Art Fund specialises in modern British painting. It is my business to know of such fine painters as Dod Proctor. She is unmistakable. And my goodness— '

Downstairs the shop doorbell rang, cutting me off. Mr Goodston made a noise indicating irritation at the possible arrival of more custom.

'If you will excuse me for one moment?'

'Of course.'

I trod carefully over the piles of books on the floor while he disappeared downstairs. The painting had an appeal that is difficult to describe. The child had thin arms and was dressed in a collared frock of the 1930s. The china on the table was blue with white spots, probably from the T. H. Green pottery. Dod Proctor deserved to be represented among the Art Fund's range of paintings well ahead of other, more fashionable women artists.

Downstairs there was a crack and a scuffle, resulting in a heavy thumping cascade of books. A voice bellowed in anger.

'Pay up! Now! Or else!'

I nipped back over the books, down the staircase and into the shop. Mr Goodston was pinned to the wall behind his desk, spectacles askew, by a fattish man in a stained suit who grasped his lapels. Another thick-set bloke stood leaning with his back to the door, hard against it so that no one could get in.

'Here, here,' I said mildly. 'What's all this about?'

Fatty let go of Mr Goodston and turned towards me with a nasty scowl. 'It's about money owing. That's what it's about. Who are you, then? The new minder?'

I raised my eyebrows at Mr Goodston, who was getting his breath back.

'Injudicious,' he gasped, ' – unfortunate – betting shop – poor horses – a temporary embarrassment – '

'Temporary!' The fat man curled his lip. 'You owe my guvnor a lot of cash and have done for a long time. Now you pay up, see, or else.'

'Or else what?' I enquired, bristles starting on the back of my neck.

The fat man faced me with a sneer. 'Or else people will get hurt. Got me, squire? Yourself included.'

My dear old father used to say that the essence of success in war is to use the utmost brutality. A military man would have added that an element of surprise helps a lot. Fatty was standing all wrong for a real professional: legs apart, arms akimbo, head thrust forward aggressively. I leant my back against a bookcase and brought my right foot up sharply, like a man punting a good up-and-under for a scrum to chase, straight into the place it would hurt most. There was a great choked-off screech and he doubled up in the middle of the floor. His chum on the door bounded forward predictably on to a straight left to the end of the nose, with gratifyingly sanguinary results. I wrenched the door open while he clasped bloodied hands to his injured hooter and propelled him through.

'Out,' I said. 'Both of you.'

The doubled-up fat one managed to hit his head on the door-jamb as I shoved him out. He turned to snarl at me painfully.

'You haven't heard the last of this,' he wheezed. 'We'll be back.'

'You tell your guvnor to collect his money legally or next time I'll shove you under a bus.' I gestured at a large red one hammering its way down Praed Street. 'Without the slightest compunction.' With a glance at a couple of entranced passers-by I went back in and slammed the door. Mr Goodston had slid down on to the chair behind his desk. Distress emanated from him.

'My dear Mr Simpson! The shame! The humiliation! I am mortified! Your kind efforts – much appreciated – awful – what would I have done – you are a dangerous man when roused, sir. But I am done, Mr Simpson, done.' He waved a hopeless hand at his desk and the racing papers. 'My downfall, sir. My downfall. Since my dear wife died . . . ' He gestured vaguely and let his hand fall dramatically to the crowded surface. It was clear that even in his financial extremities Mr Goodston had been unable to resist the lure of the turf. A detailed programme for the day's racing at Haydock Park was carefully marked in red pencil. I shook my head sadly as I picked it up.

'Mr Goodston, it is not for me to criticise your pastimes. I do not gamble, myself. I may have related to you that once, during a heavy downpour in the Nathan Road, Hong Kong, I had my palm read by an Indian.

He took one look at my hand and advised me never to gamble. Nevertheless, it is an excitement I think I can understand . . . '

I let my voice trail off. My eye had inevitably caught sight of the lists of runners. Prickles went down my spine. Fate was staring me in the eye.

'What is it, Mr Simpson?'

'It's incredible! There's a horse called Dainty Dinah running in the five thirty at Haydock Park! Fifty to one against. You haven't marked it.'

'Indeed I have not. It is a rank outsider. Rank.'

I put the paper down. I felt feverish. 'Is there a betting shop near here that you can use? I mean one where you are not a major debtor?'

He gaped at me. 'Near the station. But— '

'But me no buts, Mr Goodston. We are going to that shop now. I shall put down, on your behalf, three hundred quid on Dainty Dinah to win.'

'Mr Simpson! What is this?'

'Actually – no – yes, damn it – I shall also put fifty quid on it for myself as well. It will pay for my holiday in Cartagena with Sue.'

'Mr Simpson! Mr Simpson, please! What has possessed you? I cannot allow it! The horse cannot win! I couldn't repay you!'

'Ah, yes you could. Because the horse will win. And' – I held up a hand to restrain him – 'even if it doesn't win, you will be able to recoup the loss. It can be a loan against the books I shall buy from you. Look upon it as a payment on account. I shall easily purchase that value of books in a relatively short period. But it will be unnecessary. The horse will win.'

Mr Goodston paused. Mr Goodston is a gambling man. He blinked at me. 'But – but Mr Simpson, why? Why this sudden urge?' His expression became anxious.

'Did you sustain a knock in your imbroglio just now? You are not a gambler. I can confirm that you have told me that many times. I would never forgive myself if I were to be the cause of a horrible stumble in your forward and distinguished career. Please, Mr Simpson, why? Why?'

'I cannot tell you that just now, Mr Goodston, because I am superstitious. It would spoil the chance. Come, let us place our bets. I take it that your obligations do not amount to more than fifteen thousand pounds?'

He shook his head dumbly. My glance fell on the red cloth Vernon book, now lying on the floor. 'How much do I owe you for that?'

He picked it up and handed it to me. 'With my compliments, my dear sir. With my compliments, in return for your, er, assistance just now.'

'Thank you, Mr Goodston, but I do not expect you to give me your stock. However, there's no time to lose. We must go and place our bets quickly, before the odds shorten in.'

He gave me a wondering look. 'There is no danger of that. No danger at all.'

I practically ran him from the shop and we placed the bets. We got fifty to one without demur. Mr Goodston pocketed his receipts and I took mine for my fifty-pound flutter. I promised to phone him after the horse had won and arrange to celebrate. He looked at me strangely but said nothing; gamblers have superstitions about chains of events.

I spent that afternoon inside watching television. It was the longest afternoon of my life. By the time the five thirty at Haydock Park came on I felt as though I had been waiting in the changing-room at Twickenham before the Oxford match for five years. Dainty Dinah was a small brown horse the cameras barely noticed. They concentrated on three others. At the first bend Dainty Dinah was well back. On the far leg of the course she made up a few places. On the last bend she moved into third place. I knocked my mug of tea over onto the carpet. Down the final straight she sailed past the favourite and the second favourite. She won by three clear lengths with no possible challenges or infringements. I found that I was hoarse and must have been shouting; I rushed to the telephone but Mr Goodston's phone rang without reply. I guessed that he would have watched the race in the betting shop and was now either being given sal volatile or was in the pub, buying drinks. I downed a large gin and tonic myself. I felt like going out and kicking a hole in the big drum. I thought of Sue and decided to give her a big surprise when she got back. I was restless.

I managed to calm myself by reading the book on Vernon. It was gripping stuff. If Vernon hadn't been hampered by a blockheaded redcoat General called Wentworth he would have captured Cartagena and Latin America might have fallen into British hands. I decided that the cloth-headed Wentworth might have done us an unintentional good turn. Vernon ended up, just like Cochrane after him, at odds with the Board of Admiralty, who struck him off. I finished the book late at night; it was in good condition except for some jottings – a name and two telephone numbers – on the map endpapers, which was irritating. People mistreat books.

In the morning I breakfasted cheerfully and then nipped over to Praed Street. Mr Goodston keeps a bottle of Celebration Cream sherry in his desk for special occasions and I rather fancied a glass with him in view of events. There was a policeman standing by the door of the shop and I bade him an affable good morning. It wasn't until I'd passed him and was inside that I noticed that he'd followed me and that the interior was unaccountably full for a Sunday.

I first sighted the two bookie's men. They stood against a bookcase looking a bit sheepish. Facing them was a sturdy plain-clothes man whose occupation was obvious. Next to him stood an athletic-looking ginger-haired man who let out an exclamation at the sight of me.

'Good heavens,' I said. 'Hello, Nobby. How are you today?'

'That's 'im.' The fat heavy one pointed at me excitedly, as though justifying himself.

'Who are you?' the uniformed policeman demanded.

'It's all right,' I answered him, 'I am well acquainted with Chief Inspector Roberts.'

'That's him,' Fatty insisted again, self-righteously. 'Violent bastard, he is. Dangerous. He's your man.'

The plain-clothes man spoke. 'Are you saying that this is the man involved in your affray yesterday?'

'Yeah. That's him. Nasty piece of work. I told you. Look at him.'

The ginger-haired man let out an audible groan. I have known Nobby Roberts since we were at college together, where he played on the wing while I was a front row man, usually a prop. When he left college he went into the police force to satisfy a strong sense of social and judicial vocation. He is a very serious police officer and tends to get pompous but he's a close friend.

'Dear God,' he now said, in stricken tones, 'I don't believe it. Tim, are you really the man involved in a punch-up with these two yesterday morning on these premises? Witnessed by several passers-by?'

'I wouldn't have called it an affray, Nobby. Just seeing them off the premises, you know. They have unpleasant methods of debt collection.'

'For heaven's sake,' he snapped, 'I've just circulated your description to the entire Metropolitan Police Force.'

'You didn't have to do that, Nobby. All you had to do was phone me. I would have confessed to everything.'

He opened his mouth, closed it, opened it again, then closed it.

'Where's Mr Goodston?' I demanded.

'Mr Goodston,' the plain-clothes man said, 'was the subject of a severe attack yesterday afternoon, late, here. It was fortunate that his assailants were interrupted. As it is, he is in hospital under sedation.'

'Oh dear. Oh dear, oh dear.' I bit my lip.

Nobby Roberts glared at me before turning to the plain-clothes man. 'Take these two and get their statements,' he ordered. To the uniformed man he said, 'You stay here. Let no one in. They're still searching upstairs.' Then he wheeled on me with a grim expression. 'You – you follow me.' He stalked out of the shop and I followed him meekly down the street until we got to an Italian café where he marched in and ordered two coffees. His eyes were tinged with pink. We took a table to ourselves and I leaned across to him, confidentially.

'I say, Nobby, are things a bit quiet down at the Yard? I mean why is a big-time rozzer like you called out on a Sunday morning for a bookshop break-in? Don't suppose Gillian can be very pleased, can she?'

His eyes got a bit pinker. 'Suppose you do some explaining first, for a change? What the bloody hell are you up to? Eh?'

'Keep calm, old friend. I saw Sue off to her mother's yesterday morning and then popped in to ask for a book. While we were talking those two thugs came in and started leaning on Mr Goodston for a gambling debt. So I ejected them.'

He stared at me distractedly. 'I sometimes wonder if it's possible for me to investigate any crime in London without you getting in the way. What in hell were you after with Mr Goodston? I didn't know that front row men could read.'

'There is no need to be offensive, Nobby. I am one of Mr Goodston's regulars. I have had stuff from him on Ellen Terry and Whistler and Moreton Frewen— '

'Oh no! Oh no! The mere mention of those names fills me with dread. Not another? Oh, please. Not another?'

'Nobby, control yourself. Get a grip, man. I just wanted a book. Anyway, that was in the morning. You say he was attacked again late yesterday?'

'Yes.' He picked up his coffee and took a swig of it.

'Was that before or after he won his fifteen thousand pounds?'

Coffee spurted from him. I managed to get some napkins and mop him up while a clucking Italian matron, who had run out from behind her Gaggia machine, clapped him on the back. After he'd stopped choking and cleaned himself he glared at me, eyes red, face suffused. 'What fifteen thousand pounds?'

'The fifteen thousand he won on Dainty Dinah. The horse I backed for him in the five thirty at Haydock Park.'

A look of the most intense suspicion combined with an unattractive scarlet scowl came over his face. 'You did what?'

'I made him back a horse. It was a cert. I lent

him three hundred and it came in at fifty to one. I went with him to the betting shop to put it on. The horse won. Actually, Nobby, I had fifty quid on it myself. It'll pay for me and Sue to go on holiday. Cartagena. I'm looking forward to that. Do you know— '

'Stop! Stop right there! You never bet on horses! Never! I've been to countless dinner parties you've bored to death with that story of yours about a palm reader in Hong Kong. He told you never to gamble and you never do.'

'There is no need to be offensive, Nobby. People enjoy that story. Anyway, this was different.'

'Why?'

'Well— '

I was fated to be interrupted that weekend. A burly bloke with short hair barged in through the café door and addressed Nobby from the side of our table.

'No go, Chief. We've checked right through.' He handed Nobby a paper with a list on it. 'Still missing. And we've gone through the lot with a fine-tooth comb. Page by page.'

Nobby gave him a look that was not at all complimentary. 'It has to be there. Check again.'

'But, sir— '

'Check again! You've got to find it. Go back to the hospital as well and see if you can question Goodston. There's no time!'

The burly bloke withdrew, looking sullen. I raised my eyebrows in query but got no response from across the table. I sipped my coffee whilst thoughts could be detected seething across Nobby's face.

'God damn it,' he said, eventually.

'Anything I can help with at all?'

He gave me a sour look. Various bitter expressions

distorted his features until, at last, a resigned demeanour came over him. He muttered to himself for a moment and then spoke out loud.

'Mullarkey,' he said.

'I beg your pardon?'

'Barry Mullarkey. You may not have heard of him. He lives in St John's Wood. He's a fence. A dealer. A villain. He deals in all things illegal and stolen. Including drugs. He skipped it to Spain last week. We had an agent – a cleaner – working on the inside, in his flat. We were poised to go. The key to Mullarkey's dealings is his Swiss bank account. The Swiss have promised to co-operate but they need the details of his account. Under current drug law we can confiscate the lot. Mullarkey memorised the numbers but our agent heard that Mullarkey had written the details down in case he forgot them or for his wife to find. He is a great collector of books; every year he has to cull his collection by about a hundred volumes to allow room for new ones. Your Mr Goodston buys the cull. He did it again this year, the deal being set up just before Mullarkey skipped it. The books are upstairs in the shop right now.'

'Ah. Nobby— '

'Wait! Will you let me finish! By mistake, Mullarkey's henchman, a dumb cluck called Foster, let go the book that contains the details of the Swiss account written in it. Mullarkey gave him hell on the phone from Spain. Hence the attack on Mr Goodston: to get the book back. We scared them off but they got away. We need those account numbers and we've no time to lose.'

'So the fifteen thousand pounds was nothing to do with it?'

'Of course not! Stop interrupting! As far as I know

Mr Goodston must still have his betting receipts safe and sound. He seems to be very meticulous; his records and cataloguing are good enough to satisfy even a VAT inspector. All those books of Mullarkey's are listed and we've been through every page of every one of them without success. All except one, that is. There's one missing.'

'Ah. That would be *The Angry Admiral*, by Cyril Hughes Hartmann, Nobby. Published by Heinemann in 1953.'

This time I thought the coffee was going to spurt from his ears. The Italian matron rushed out from behind her Gaggia machine in quite a state to thump him on the back as I mopped him up. The gist of her comments was that he was giving her coffee a bad name. That didn't please him, either.

'How the hell did you know that was the missing title? We've been combing that bloody shop all morning. We need those numbers! Only we have the list of books that Goodston bought off Mullarkey. My men went to hospital with him and he told them where to find it, even though he was very shaky. You can't have seen it!'

'Of course I haven't seen it. I bought the book off Mr Goodston yesterday. At least, technically I haven't actually bought it because I haven't paid for it yet, so I don't suppose Mr Goodston has registered the sale in his books. What with two assaults in one day I expect he forgot to tell you, but I've got it.'

'Why? *For Pete's sake, why?*'

'Nobby, you must calm yourself. I keep trying to tell you, I'm going to Cartagena on holiday. So— '

'Where the hell is that book?' he shouted. His eyes were bright red.

'At home. And it's funny you should mention it

because someone has spoiled the endpapers by putting a name and two sets of numbers right in the old map of the Caribbean that— '

I got no further. He was on his feet, bellowing. He grabbed me by the lapels. He ran me from the shop whilst hurling money at the Italian matron. He bellowed even louder when he got outside and a police car came squeaking up like a terrified pet. He roared the address of my flat in Onslow Gardens at the driver and his mate before we were scattered across the back seat as the car shot off. I had to grab a handle to steady myself.

'Cartagena.' His voice was thick. 'Cartagena? What do you keep raving on about Cartagena for?'

'A holiday, Nobby. I was interested in the Vernon connection. *The Angry Admiral* is a book about Admiral Vernon. I've been trying to explain to you. Remember Jeremy White's uncle, Sir Richard? His hobby was visiting the sites of the battles of the Hundred Years War. A perfectly innocent pastime with gastronomic perks. I thought I might do something similar in South America. It's not unknown, you know. An ambassador called John Ure did a book on Morgan— '

'Eccentric.' His furious voice cut me off. 'No, not just eccentric, mad. You're mad. Cartagena? In Colombia? You'll get yourself and Sue slaughtered.'

The car careered into the Old Brompton Road on two wheels. I shot him a glance. 'What about you? I fear for your health, you know, Nobby. If you go cutting short your coffee breaks and being driven like this you'll get severe dyspepsia and— '

'Shut up! Just shut up!'

We hurtled to a halt outside my flat. He and the front man were out before we stopped moving. They shot up the stairs three at a time. I skipped along behind thinking they'd have to wait for me to open up but I was wrong. The door was open and they shot through like a pair of ferrets. I heard a great bellow from Nobby.

'Foster!'

The inside of my flat was somewhat deranged. Most of my books were on the floor. By the time I entered four men were struggling fiercely across the centre carpet. Nobby was twisting the arm behind a medium-sized fellow in a sweater and jeans whilst his uniformed man was having a lot of trouble with a bigger bloke in a corduroy jacket. I leapt in to help before the flat got wrecked. I have to admit that I was very indignant; when the two men were handcuffed and out of the place I addressed Nobby with some irritation.

'Who gave them my address? Eh?'

'You idiot! That was Mullarkey's dumb assistant, Foster, but the other one is his very dangerous right-hand man. With the spectacle you made of yourself at Goodston's yesterday it can't have been all that difficult for them to trace you. Now – where the *hell* is that book?'

It was by the bedside, where I'd left it. I handed it to Nobby and he stared at the name and numbers in the back until, for the first time that day, his face started to relax. 'Thank the Lord for that,' he said. 'I'll keep this.'

'Hang on! That's my book! I want it for my holiday. You've got your numbers.'

He stuck his face close to mine. 'This book,' he said, 'is evidence. You can have it back once a successful prosecution and sequestration of funds has taken place.'

'Oh, that's great! I like that! That's the thanks I get, is it? A wrecked flat and my book purloined by ungrateful policemen. I don't suppose you'll even offer to help clear this up before Sue gets back this afternoon?'

He grinned savagely. 'The rest of my Sunday is going to be quite busy enough without helping poor little Timmy to hide this lot from Sue. Serves you right. Teach you to keep out of trouble and not to hit bookies' men, not even in a good cause.'

And with that the ungrateful blighter went out. I sat down to survey the mess until his head popped round the door again.

'By the way,' he said, 'you never told me how you knew that horse was going to win.'

'That,' I replied, with some hauteur, 'is between Mr Goodston and me. You've behaved very badly and since you find my stories so boring you can jolly well wait until you hand over that book before you hear this one.'

He made a face at me and left. It didn't take me all that long to clear up because most of the displacement was books. I picked up an auction catalogue and went off to Mr Goodston's well before Sue's train was due back. Knowing how most hospitals work these days I guessed he'd be home again and he was. He sat behind his desk with a piece of sticking plaster gummed to his forehead and a bruise below one eye, but his manner was jaunty.

'My very dear Mr Simpson! My saviour!' He waved his betting slips at me. 'You are incredible, sir! A maestro! How did you do it?'

'Are you all right, Mr Goodston?'

'As you see: battered but unbowed. And much wealthier. Thanks to you.'

'Good.' I sat down next to him.

'Please, Mr Simpson, can you now tell me? Please? Why that horse?'

I grinned at him. 'It was extraordinary. That Dod

Proctor of yours upstairs of the little girl; she features in several of her paintings. I have often wondered who that wistful child was. Until this week.' I held up a Christie's catalogue and opened it in front of him. 'Sold for £46,000 on 2 March 1989. Lot 95. A painting by Dod Proctor, RA. Possibly a record price.' I opened the pages further so that he could see the coloured illustration of a painting of an adolescent girl sitting by a window, looking at a red book, with cloth binding. His eyes bulged a little before he glanced involuntarily up to the ceiling, in the direction of the room upstairs where his painting of the same girl, somewhat younger, hung on the wall. Then he looked down to the title of the painting sold at Christie's:

Dinah, Reading.

'It came in yesterday morning. The catalogue and price list, sent on from the office. I never saw such a cert in my life, not in a bookshop or anywhere else.'

Mr Goodston reached into his desk. Mr Goodston pulled out a full bottle of Celebration Cream sherry.

'Mr Simpson,' he croaked, 'would you care for a glass – no, damn it, for a beaker at least – of Celebration Cream?'

Pray Tell Me, Sir, Whose Dog Are You?

by Jennie Melville

The small figure seated on the large Chippendale sofa was murmuring (but perfectly to be heard since audibility is the politeness of kings) gentle words of thanks for the rescue of a favourite dog.

She was wearing a soft harebell blue tweed suit that Charmian envied passionately. She herself might be a high-powered and successful policewoman but she still loved clothes. Chief Superintendent Charmian Daniels, whether in uniform or out of it (and she had done her term as a uniformed WPC before rising high into the CID force, and now occupying a specially created post in the Met), had never allowed herself to forget she was a woman.

'It was nothing, ma'am.' She had found a precious kidnapped dog. Who could do less as a loyal subject? The dog had bitten her, but what matter? He had, one heard, bitten more illustrious hands.

A delicate hand, adorned with a huge sapphire, caressed the returned animal's ear.

'Do you have a dog yourself?'

'Er . . . no, ma'am.'

A faint, sad look crossed her interlocutor's face.

'I did have, of course,' said Charmian quickly. 'But it died.' Twenty odd years ago, but no need to say so.

'Ah, but you must have one. You don't shoot?'

'Er, no, ma'am.' Shoot what, she asked herself? I have been an authorised 'shot' for some time, I may carry a gun. I have shot a man. Never a grouse nor pheasant, though. Eaten some. One or two poached, I suspect, ma'am, from your royal coverts.

A soft smile. 'I am sure we can find you one.' She rose. The interview was over.

'I will send one from the new litter. Not a gun dog, just as a pet.'

Just for a moment, it looked as though she would say something else, but she did not. Not the sort of subject to be broached. But there was a look in her eyes.

'The child?' she might just have been going to say. 'Is there anything new about the child?' It was certainly there, one thought, at the back of her mind. And it was a question being much asked locally.

A town child. It was in all the papers. One of those stories so common and so fearful.

A child, Fiona Cofrey, a pretty, unremarkable child, but much loved, some six years old, well grown and sophisticated for her years, who had been last seen cycling through that ancient royal town of Windsor on the Thames, and then was gone. Even her bicycle was missing.

A witness had said she was pedalling hard and that her face was red. She had had a quarrel with her younger brother and her pocket money had been docked. The Cofrey family were loving, but discipline was firm.

A week later, the child being still missing, Benjy arrived, labelled, and with his pedigree (which needless to say, was noble) and with his Kennel Club Registration. He had had all possible immunisations, he was a healthy boy. Somewhat short in the leg, with a large waving tail and liquid, loving eyes.

You could see why he was not a gun dog, nor ever would be one. He was far too loving. He would have been rescuing the birds and licking them back to life. Killing was not what he was made for.

He attached himself with anxious devotion to Charmian. She had the feeling that she would never be alone again.

'He's a loony, miss,' said the gaitered man in green tweed who had driven him over in a green van. 'Ought to have been put down. But there it is, we're not allowed. All got to go to a good home.'

At least I'm a good home, thought Charmian. By Royal Appointment.

Although tender-hearted, blood will tell, so Benjy retained some gun dog instincts: he retrieved everything. He preferred vegetable and mineral materials. Stones, wood, paper, the odd feather provided it had long been divorced from the bird.

When the cat Muff, who had no such feelings (and who was suspected of having quietly established a second home for herself, as cats so often did when cross), brought in a bird, Benjy's wails were long and loud.

He made a friend of Charmian's neighbours. Birdie Peacock and Winifred Eagle. The two women shared a house in Abigail Place, a nest they jokingly said, their garden abutting on Charmian's own in Maid of Honour Row. The house belonged to Winifred but her friend had joined her a year ago.

Charmian had found Winifred Eagle a daunting neighbour at first, but Winifred had softened a lot lately, and Charmian had come to appreciate the goodness and gentleness (combined with great intellectual energy) of both women.

Birdie and Winifred were ladies of late middle age and independent income with a wide range of interests. Winifred had founded a chapter of white witches and when this foundered because of lack of young recruits (You do need a few young witches; it's like nuns, they mustn't all be old. Winifred's words), they had tried homeopathy, aromatherapy and Transcendental Meditation. Then at a large gathering at Avebury with like-minded searchers after truth, they had met a tall bearded man who read their auras and told them of their futures and of their pasts by staring into a bowl of water on which floated fragrant oils. He told them about reincarnation, but he must not tell them too much, not all at once, he said; they had to be ready.

Birdie thought she was ready now, but he had told her she was a 'Gatekeeper'. An old spirit who kept the gate to the past open.

From her windows Charmian could see the towers of the castle with the Royal Standard fluttering.

Within a short walking distance over the Thames was the King's College of our Lady of Eton Beside Windsor, founded by that most devout of English Kings, Henry VI.

Charmian used to walk across the bridge to exercise Benjy on a stretch of woodland and grass overlooking the river and by a very old and small church dedicated to St Frideswyde. The church was older than Windsor Castle and immeasurably older than Eton College, having been built by pious Anglo-Saxons anxious to keep the Viking invaders at bay. Almost all the low, old English construction with its little squat tower remained. Every year seemed to make it sink deeper into the ground as if the years were swallowing it up.

Birdie and Winifred Eagle sometimes came on these walks. Winifred being, as well as a member of so many other faiths, a communicating member of the Anglican Church, and claimed St Frideswyde as her patron saint. She treated the church as a kind of club. Clubability was what really interested her. Birdie was more naturally a believer. But she liked her faiths to be interesting and personalised with For Birdie written all over them.

Both ladies were keen animal lovers. Winifred had owned a cat, now dead, but thought by her to have had supernatural powers. The late Benedict was greatly missed and both Winifred and Birdie were prepared to patronise Benjy. They thought the name meant something: Ben into Benjy. Benedict might have come back to them, some cats do go around disguised as dogs. This is a truth guessed at by some but not widely known. It is for reasons of protection and varies, so it is claimed, from town to town. This might be the case with Benjy. There was something about him certainly.

'He's a very strange little dog,' said Birdie. 'He's forever bringing me little presents. Puts them at my feet.'

'Nothing too alarming, I hope?'

'Oh no, bits of this and bits of that. But he has such a manner, almost bows to me.'

Ah well, thought Charmian. Once you've lived a court life . . .

'So delicately done.'

The three of them were walking the dog. They came up to the patch of rough ground bordering the churchyard of St Frideswyde. On the other side of it was a row of little houses which looked fully as old as the church.

Once a quiet deserted spot, there were usually a few people about now. Onlookers. Sightseers. Staring, looking. Occasionally taking a photograph.

'She was last seen near here,' said Birdie. 'On this road. But you know that.'

'The child?'

'Yes, a woman who was weeding in the churchyard saw her cycling along the road.'

Charmian looked at the churchyard. Still a lot of weeds.

'The child shouldn't have been allowed to cycle round on her own. They say she was always about the town, going everywhere she fancied.' Winifred was critical. 'I blame the parents.'

'Do you think they ill-treated her?' asked Birdie, full of ready sympathy. 'You hear so much about child abuse these days.'

'Not enough discipline,' pronounced Winifred crisply. 'Parents out at work all day, two girls and a boy, granny left in charge.'

'Perhaps they loved the little boy more,' said Birdie. 'Some parents do and children do mind unfairness so.' She said it sadly.

'Too late to be cross now.' Charmian leaned down to release Benjy from his leash. Now he could run freely.

'She'd had a quarrel with her brother and gone off. She was an independent little creature, they all say so.' Birdie explained it.

'You didn't know her, Birdie?' asked Charmian.

Birdie shook her head. 'Of course not. Children always seem frightened of me. I don't know why.' She spoke sadly.

Charmian thought she knew why. Her friend Birdie was tall and thin with a flutter of clothes and she had a clear grey gaze like glass which could be alarming. Also she had a local reputation, not undeserved, as a witch. Charmian wondered what sort of aura the seer had given her. She couldn't make a guess at the colour, perhaps no colour, pale and shining and waving like water.

'There was a murder in that house at the end,' said Winifred, nodding towards the last of the little houses. 'When I was a girl, just after the end of the war. Remember, Birdie?'

Birdie shook her head, looking nervous. 'Not really.'

'Caused quite a schemozzle.'

'Did it?' Charmian was fascinated by the word schemozzle; she had never heard anyone say it aloud before, had not thought anyone ever could.

'More than one murder, really. Chap came back from the war, killed his wife, two children and himself. Quite an ordinary sort of murder, really.'

'Oh, would you say so?'

'Quite common, I should think. Was then, anyway. Chaps coming back from the war, a bit strung up. Suspicious. Not without reason sometimes. He thought she'd been unfaithful while he was away. Expect she had been as a matter of fact. No one would live in that house for ages afterwards. Stayed empty. Remember that, Birdie?'

'I remember that,' said Birdie obediently.

'I'm surprised you don't remember the murder.'

'I must have been away that summer.'

'Yes, it was summer, you've got that right,' said Winifred in some triumph.

Charmian did not understand the slight tension, but it was there. She broke into it: 'Oh look, Benjy's bringing you some flowers.'

Benjy, left to his own devices, had dug up some vigorous-looking trailing weeds, cow parsley and meadowsweet and some other flowers, and was now walking towards Birdie with the leaves and flowers trailing from his mouth.

He laid them at Birdie's feet and looked up at her hopefully.

'I'm afraid I usually give him a small sweetie,' confessed Birdie with an apologetic face. She put her hand in her pocket.

'Ruining him,' said Winifred.

'I'm just as weak with him myself,' Charmian admitted. 'He absolutely adores chocolate and I can't get him to eat a dog biscuit.'

Birdie patted Benjy on the head, slipping him something small from her pocket at the same time.

A grateful Benjy sped back to the bed of meadowsweet and cow parsley and started an enthusiastic excavation.

'That's cornflower and that's forget-me-not,' said Winifred, examining his offering to Birdie. 'Not a wild flower. Someone must have planted it.'

'Might have seeded itself,' said Charmian.

'Not cornflower. You need a root or a cutting.' Winifred was a gardener of some local repute. Even her weeds were grown to provide medicines or tisanes.

Benjy was working away enthusiastically with his front feet as well as his teeth, occasionally tossing a spray of vegetation over his shoulder as he dug.

He was exposing stone, worked stones, laid neatly each upon each to form a small mound, no more than four feet or so long and rounded over, and covered with earth and vegetation.

Tucked away in the rough ground by the churchyard, so overgrown, it was obscure, easily passed over.

Benjy had dislodged earth from the front and was now working away at it with his paddy feet. Eyes bright, mouth full of foliage, he wagged his tail.

'Wait a minute, Benjy. Hold on.' Charmian took his collar and drew him away.

She bent down, almost on her knees. When you looked closely you could see that the stones were, in fact, not worked stone, but pieces of rock and broken cement, carefully chosen to match.

As she looked, she saw that the mound had a kind of mouth. This mouth was blocked with a large piece of stone which Benjy had partly dislodged.

She touched it, moving it gently aside. A puff of damp, dead air, smelling very faintly of mortality puffed out towards her.

Charmian leaned back on her heels, clipping Benjy's leash on to his collar. He was straining to get forward, snuffling eagerly. She could see inside a tiny hollow space where earth and decayed vegetation had fallen. But she could also see something else, something small and dark and brown.

'Hold the dog for me.' Her voice was sharp as she handed the leash over to Birdie and knelt down for a closer look.

A bundle wrapped in what might have been white cloth but now was brown.

All three of them were crouching there now, eyes intent.

'What is it?' said Winifred.

'I think it's a tomb,' Birdie whispered.

Charmian, who was nearest, studied what she saw. Something was sticking out of the bottom of the bundle.

'A little tomb.' Birdie seemed to have difficulty with the words.

'Yes.' What Charmian saw were small bones.

'Human?'

'Small bones,' said Charmian shortly. 'I didn't look closer.'

'A baby?'

'Possibly.' Could it be a baby? Or a child, a curled-up child?

The small body had been wrapped in a blanket. A circle of flowers had been placed on top. By some freak of local conditions, they were still recognisable as flowers. Dried, shrivelled, colourless and yet preserved.

Flowers planted on top of the tomb, flowers inside the tomb, like a buried pharoah. There might even be remains of a fresh bouquet, she thought as she looked around.

'Who would bury a child like that?' said Birdie.

'Many people.' Charmian stood up. 'Many people.'

Winifred said, 'Is it, can it be, the missing little girl?'

'No, whoever it is has been dead a long time. Years.' And buried for years.

'Murdered?'

'We can't know that yet.'

Birdie, who had been going whiter and whiter, staggered against Charmian.

'We must get her a taxi,' said Winifred. She looked round wildly, as if expecting one to appear across the grass. Benjy barked with excitement and leapt up at Birdie.

'We'll try in one of the houses over there,' Charmian nodded. 'Use their telephone.'

Charmian supported her friend towards the row of small houses. By common accord they avoided the house in which murder had been done, and tried the house next door. The small front garden was neat and well tended with a well-planted border of blue and red and pink blossoms lining the path.

The door was opened by a pretty, grey-haired woman, not young, wearing a flowered cotton dress. She gave a quick sympathetic sound at the sight of the ashen Birdie leaning against Charmian.

'Could I telephone for a taxi, please?'

'Of course, come in.' The woman opened the door wider. 'Has there been an accident?'

Charmian was evasive. She didn't want to mention what they had found. 'No, my friend just feels faint.'

'I'm better now, I could walk home,' said Birdie without conviction.

Benjy had pushed his way in ahead of them, still trailing bits of blossom and leaves.

'The telephone's over here.' The woman pointed to a table in the hall. There was a seat next to it on to which she helped Birdie. Benjy sat himself at her feet and looked around with interest. Anything was grist to his mill. 'What a nice little dog.'

'Yes, he is, or most of the time,' agreed Charmian dialling the number of the Eton and Slough Taxi Service. She used it a lot and knew the number well. There was a large, silver-framed photograph on the telephone table. A round face, with a bow in the hair, frilled dress, and white socks above buttoned shoes. 'What a pretty child.'

'Yes, my daughter.' The woman smiled happily. 'She's grown up now, of course.' She pointed to a picture on the further wall. 'That's her.'

A smiling face, a mini skirt and a beehive hairstyle. A lovely face, charmingly made up and posed.

'A beauty,' said Charmian. There was another picture of a bride just visible on the sitting-room wall beyond as well as a photograph of a baby in a pram by the front door. Then a rather blurred snapshot of a child and an older boy on a bike. Daughter was well represented, if they were all of her.

'Children of her own now, I expect,' said Birdie.

'As yet, no.' She looked at Birdie, at whose feet Benjy was lolling, mouth open, tongue out. 'Can I get you a drink of water?'

'No, thank you.'

'Taxi's on its way,' announced Charmian. Benjy moved across to Charmian and panted heavily. He had a feeling there was food and drink about.

'Or perhaps the dog?'

'I expect he'd like one.'

A bowl of water was produced for Benjy who had drained and licked the dish as if he had never tasted water before, completing the job just as the taxi arrived. Charmian and Winifred helped their friend into the car.

'Oh, thank you, Mrs . . . ' she hesitated.

'Mrs Palmer.' The woman had a sweet smile.

As she turned to thank their hostess, she had the impression, surprising to her when the woman herself was so neat, that the recesses of the hall and the sitting-room beyond were not as tidy as she might have expected. Objects seemed to lie on the floor, a hint of litter.

When she had Winifred and Birdie safely deposited at home, Charmian telephoned the local police station not far from her house to report the grave.

'No, not the missing child, these are bones. Old bones. Not Roman or prehistoric or anything like that. Say thirty years or so at a guess.'

'Right. We'll take a look.'

'Anything fresh on the missing child?'

'Not a sign of her, she could be anywhere. She went off once before, and got as far as Slough, all down those busy roads; wouldn't think it, would you?

Kids can be amazing. But . . . ' he hesitated.

'But what?'

'A white sock has been found in a ditch not far from where she was last seen. Blood on it.'

'Could belong to any child.'

'True. But close by there was a handkerchief. That has been positively identified by the kid's mother. Blood on that, as well.'

'Doesn't look too good, does it?'

Charmian digested this information, then she said slowly, 'Just one thing, and it can't have anything to do with the disappearance of the child, but I thought I could just make out, chiselled on one stone of that tomb, the word MARY.'

Mary, there couldn't be any connection with a long-dead Mary and Fiona Cofrey, could there?

As she put the telephone down Charmian looked at Benjy: he was still trailing flowers which he must have gathered as he left Mrs Palmer's house. A blue tendril hung from his jaws as he tenderly chewed a leaf.

'I wonder if I'm feeding you right,' worried Charmian, as she disentangled Benjy from his decoration. There seemed to be a deficiency in his diet that demanded vegetation.

Shutting her cat Muff in one room and Benjy in another, she walked round the corner to tell Birdie and Winifred Eagle that she had informed the local police about the tomb and would let them know what happened.

She found Birdie on her own. Winifred had gone shopping.

Collecting gossip, more likely, Charmian thought. Winifred Eagle had a keen ear for news.

But it gave Charmian a chance to talk to Birdie alone. Something about Birdie needed dealing with.

'Why were you so upset when we found that tomb?' Better, after all, to be blunt.

Birdie swallowed. 'It goes back a long time to something that happened then. I've never told anyone. But I think Winifred suspects. She made those remarks about the summer of the murders.'

'Nothing to do with that, is it, Birdie?' Hard to imagine Birdie mixed up in a common murder. Something exotic, just possibly, but not the crime as described by Winifred Eagle.

'No, not that. But I did kill. Not meaning to.'

Charmian waited. 'That summer?' she prompted. 'Just after the war? Had you been away?' An evacuee? Or in the Forces, a Waaf or a Wren. She was just about old enough.

Birdie smiled. 'I'd like to have been a Wren. But I never left home. I stayed to help my father with his printing works.'

'Oh, the Python Press.'

'It is now, it wasn't then. Just an ordinary printing shop. But a high-class trade, you know. We did work for the castle.'

Birdie paused before going on.

'Perhaps I should have got away; it was just after the war, I could have gone, joined something. Girls did do that. But the war was over and my father said he needed me, couldn't manage now my mother was dead. We were next door to the barracks. Such handsome men, the Guards, you know . . . Korea, he was killed there. Anyway I found I was pregnant.'

'Oh, Birdie.' Charmian could imagine the situation.

'Girls didn't have much they could do about it then. No abortion service. Oh, one heard about back-street abortionists, but girls like me didn't know how to find someone like that. So you just hung on as long as you could and then you went away and stayed with an aunt or kind friend and had the child adopted when it was born. If you were brave you stayed home and faced it all. I wasn't brave. I went away, but I never really had the child. Well, not alive, about six months it was, a bit less. I was ill and that was that. You could say I was lucky.'

'I wouldn't say that, Birdie.'

'But you see, sometimes, I think, well, perhaps I killed the child. It was inside me and I killed it. In a way, I did. Or my body did it for me. And I have nightmares sometimes that I bury a dead child . . . '

She took a deep breath before going on.

'So when we found that tomb, I thought: this is it, I really did do it, not just in a nightmare but for real. Do you think I did?'

'Not you, Birdie.' Charmian touched her friend's hands. 'Not you.'

For a moment they sat in silence, then Birdie dried her eyes. 'Let's have a cup of tea. Or better still, sherry.'

'Or better still, whisky. You're talking to a graduate of Glasgow, remember.'

Over whisky, and Birdie and Winifred kept a good malt, Birdie said, 'I feel braver now. By the way, Winifred thinks that the house we went in may have been the one the murders took place in after all.'

'I wonder if she's imagining that?' said Charmian thoughtfully.

'If she did, I'm not surprised, there was an atmosphere about that house.'

'Yes, there was. I noticed it too. And I wondered what it was.'

She thought about the row of houses, neat and quiet, and then concentrated on that particular house, just as quiet, but possibly not so neat.

Inside, the house was crowded with the photographs of the daughter. She thought about those photographs of a pretty child and beautiful daughter. There was something worrying about them.

'Birdie, why did you say what you did about the daughter having children?'

Birdie took a deep swig of whisky. 'Saw a toy in the hall.'

'I saw that too, without taking it in. Just litter, I thought, but they were toys. A toy car. A wooden train. I remember now. As though children might be playing there. No voices, though.'

'Not then.'

'What do you mean?'

'What I said. No, not then. Might have been later. When we'd left.'

'What are you saying?'

'I just had the feeling that there was talking going on in the background, waiting to burst out when we'd gone.'

'I think we're being a bit mad, don't you?'

'No,' said Birdie, pouring some more whisky. 'But I think it's just as well we are having this conversation while Winifred is out of the way. Now there is someone who can be mad.'

Charmian went home and released Benjy. 'Come on, out with you. I supposed you'd better finish the walk you never had.'

Benjy seemed quite happy to retrace his footsteps the way they had gone before.

The sun was still shining on the old church, but it was a golden, evening sun now, with a hint of the approach of night. A belt of dark clouds stretched across the sky to the west. Even as they walked across the grass to where Mrs Palmer lived, a police car was drawing up in the road and a uniformed figure was making its way through the rough grass to the tomb.

A man was gardening in the first terrace house, which might or might not be the house of several murders. He was a sturdy old man who looked as though he could put bad memories to flight, even if he knew murder had taken place in his house. Probably he did, he so wise and knowing.

'Nice dog you've got there,' he said over his hedge. 'I dare say I could work out who bred him, too.' He gave a deep cheerful laugh. 'Got one myself, you can't mistake the look. See one, you've seen the lot. It's the legs.'

Charmian was too tactful to comment on this.

'Have you lived here long?' she asked.

'Long enough.'

'I heard . . . ' she hesitated. 'Was there something about a murder here?'

'Oh, you heard that, did you? Shouldn't believe all you hear.' He bent to his digging.

'It's not true then?'

'Not denying it.'

He went on with his garden work, but somehow not releasing her.

'Visiting Mrs Palmer?' He had bright inquisitive eyes.

'Just to say thank you for a service she did me.'

'Some activity over there,' and he nodded towards the police car.

'I didn't notice,' lied Charmian.

'Reckon they'll find Fiona there?'

'No.'

'I don't reckon so either.' He gave her a sharp alert look and went back to his gardening.

'Nice flowers you've got in your garden,' said Charmian politely. He went in for geraniums, red and white, in firm displays. She preferred Mrs Palmer's cornflowers.

Flowers in the garden, flowers in the tomb. Flowers on the tomb, withered but newly picked. Cornflowers and forget-me-nots and daisies.

Mrs Palmer opened the door. 'Oh, it's you.' Over Charmian's shoulder her eyes took in the policeman walking round the tomb. She did not say anything but her gaze flicked nervously back to Charmian. 'Can I do anything?'

Always polite, Charmian thought.

'I wanted to say thank you for helping us just now. My friend was upset.'

'I saw. Poor lady.' Mrs Palmer was unobtrusively looking at the police activity across the way.

'Can I come in?'

Benjy had already surged forward so that it was easy for Charmian. Mrs Palmer offered no resistance, but she did not offer a welcome.

The hall and sitting-room were tidy now, if indeed they had ever been untidy.

Charmian looked again at the pictures of the daughter. A tiny baby in a swaddling shawl in the pram. That child could be anyone. But surely that child in the buttoned shoes could not be the same as the girl with the beehive hairstyle? The bones were wrong. And the girl with the backcombed hair could not be the bride whose picture was just visible on the sitting-room wall.

Because Charmian recognised the girl with the helmet of hair as a model girl of the sixties, and she thought she knew the bride. Hadn't she been a star in a TV series?

One daughter, or several? Or none at all.

'Could we have a talk?' she asked.

Mrs Palmer eyed her nervously. 'What about?'

'Your daughter?'

Silence.

'You have got one?'

'Why are you asking these questions? What is it to do with you?'

'The reason my friend was taken ill was that we found a burial across the way in the bushes. A small tomb.' She looked at Benjy. 'The dog found it. He got himself festooned with a wreath of dead flowers. Cornflowers and forget-me-nots. There was a wreath in the tomb. Flowers inside on the body, others growing outside on the tomb.' She added, 'Recent flowers in the wreath. Someone was still mourning. Was that you, Mrs Palmer?'

No answer.

'You have cornflowers in your garden. Benjy collected some again and I noticed.' Charmian watched the woman's hands moving restlessly. 'I don't think you have a daughter. Or not any longer. Only a fantasy you have made up to live with.'

Mrs Palmer covered her eyes. 'Go away. It's nothing to do with you. What are you, a social worker or from the NHS?'

Her flat, dull tone suggested to Charmian that the woman had had experience of both these agencies at some time in her life.

'I have a reason. Was your daughter called Mary?'

'Yes,' the words were a mere whisper. 'Mary, my baby. Please leave me alone.'

'Did you kill your child, Mrs Palmer, and then bury her?'

There was a long moment of silence. 'You're right about the pictures. But they have comforted me. You, see, that is what she would have been like. I think so,' she said in faltering voice. 'I do believe that. If she had lived. In spite of what they said.'

'What did they say?'

'That she would never be normal, never grow up. Not really grow up.'

'Is that why you killed her?'

'I didn't kill her,' said Mrs Palmer, as if resigned. 'Who said she was dead? She just didn't grow up. Like they said she might not. I think it was the fault of that house next door. There was a murder there while I was carrying her. Did something to her. That's what I put it down to. Not my fault in spite of what my husband said. I didn't pass anything on.'

'Who is it in the grave? Whom did you bury?'

'Why the dog, of course. It was a stray, a poor little bitch and my Mary loved it, called it Mary. Got confused sometimes. "Was that when I was a dog, Mummy?" she said once. You had to laugh.'

Charmian was silent in her turn.

'So when it died I buried it myself, and mourned for my Mary. I couldn't mourn the other Mary, because she doesn't know me any more. I suppose you could say she has died, far away in a home where she never should have gone. You shouldn't do that to a dog, I said to my Jim, but he made me.'

'Jim?'

'My husband. Well, he was. Dead himself now, poor fellow. I don't mean to be hard on him. He did try to do his best for us all. But he didn't see things the right way.'

She stood up. 'Well, now you've got it. I hope you are satisfied.'

Outside in the garden, Charmian collected her thoughts. Nothing there about Fiona Cofrey after all. Not even a dead child, just a dead dog.

At the gate, she saw the old man next door still at his gardening.

'Had your talk then?'

'Yes,' Charmian gave him a smile. He was going to talk, she could tell. Just give him the opportunity.

'Nice lady, Mrs Palmer. Had a hard life.'

'Yes, sad about the daughter, isn't it?'

He stopped his work. 'Daughter? Dunno about a daughter. Never seen a daughter.'

'There was one once,' said Charmian.

'A son. There's a son.'

'I didn't know that.'

'Not there all the time. She couldn't manage. Hasn't got all his marbles,' he said tolerantly. 'Comes home for holidays. Doesn't like it. You ought to get him someone to play with I said.' He leaned on his spade. 'He's there now, I think. Not that I've seen him. I make a point of never seeing kids, you're safer that way. But I've heard voices. I think the kid must be a ventriloquist.'

He was telling her something. Charmian stared at him, then dragging Benjy, she turned back. This time, she did not ring the front door but walked round the back. She looked in through the kitchen window and then pushed open the door and went in.

A girl child was sitting on the floor playing with a train set with a youth, a young man, perhaps even older than that but his face was plump and childlike. He was singing tunelessly to himself as they played. The little girl had a bandage on her knee.

Mrs Palmer, who was standing at the kitchen with a kettle in her hand, stared back at Charmian.

'So there you are, Fiona,' said Charmian. 'Fell off your bike and hurt your knee, I see. I suppose Mrs Palmer bound it up for you? Well, it's time for you to go home.'

The child turned a blank, cold blue stare on her. 'Oh, no, I'm not going home. I've come here often before. Often. Mrs Palmer says I can, she says I'm welcome. No, I'm not going back to them. I don't like my mother. I prefer it here.'

She turned back to her game, a little cat who had found an alternative home where the food was better and the petting fonder.

Charmian did all that was necessary in the way of telephoning the police, and waiting until everything was tidied up.

There were tears. 'It isn't true Fiona has stayed here before,' Mrs Palmer explained. 'But I met her sometimes on her outings, yes, more than once and gave her a little something to buy some chocolate. She likes chocolate.'

'A wee bawbie,' thought Charmian, the Scot, 'for a wee sweetie.' Adding to herself, I wouldn't trust that child further than I could see her. She's out for Fiona, first, last and all the time.

'Just this time . . . ' Mrs Palmer stumbled out her explanation. 'I thought why shouldn't she be mine? And my boy, he did need a playmate.'

A touch of ruthlessness on both sides, Charmian thought. It was one of those stories you never saw through to the bottom. One of life's strange little offerings upon which it was better not to dwell. She hoped she never came across Fiona in adult life, but it seemed to her entirely possible she might do, a criminal in the making.

'Don't cry too much, Mrs Palmer. Nor you, child.' Fiona had joined in the weeping too. Only the big boy was calm-eyed and without understanding. 'Dry your eyes, Fiona.' Because, after all, they were only crocodile tears.

Then she went home taking Benjy with her. He had the hangdog air of one who had never had the promised walk but accepted what had happened as due if unexplained punishment. If a dog was wrong, a dog was wrong, you never really got to know why. It was life.

On the way home, Charmian met Birdie.

'You look gloomy,' she said to Charmian.

'I was thinking about the terribleness of children.'

'Worse than parents?'

'Sometimes. Sometimes much worse.' She was thinking of the ruthless Fiona. The Cofreys sounded such a nice, normal family, but there must be something very wrong going on inside the group. Or do all normal families have a monster inside, tunnelling to get out?

Then she looked at Birdie, who seemed much brighter than when last seen. 'Maybe you got out of it better than you thought, Birdie.'

Birdie was excited, words on the point of bursting forth.

'I've just had a talk with Mr Dalrymple.' Mr D was her guru, her mystic leader. 'He is very good on the telephone. I'm allowed to make a call, I have special permission, only in a time of real need, you understand.'

Charmian nodded. It had been that sort of a day.

But Birdie looked radiant. 'He said the time had come when he was allowed to tell me who I had been. In my first life, I mean. Before he had been forbidden, now he could tell me. I always knew I was royal.' Birdie's head went up high.

'Oh, Birdie.' Charmian was amused but careful not to show it.

'I had been given hints. I thought it might be Cleopatra, or possibly Mary Stuart.' Was there a faint hint of disappointment in her voice that beauty as well as sovereignty had not been on offer? 'I knew it was a tragic figure . . . '

Charmian waited.

'Boudicca. I was Queen Boudicca.' She nodded. 'It's her proper name. Not Boadicea as I used to call her at school.'

To Charmian's eyes her friend looked very unlike a warlike Celtic queen.

Birdie said, 'There's only one thing missing: Angus Dalrymple says he sees me with a dog. A royal dog.'

Her eyes met Charmian's, met Benjy's, hopefully; Benjy looked hopefully back.

Charmian said, 'I can do something about that, Birdie.' Should you give away a present? She made up her mind: Benjy deserved his proper place in the world: in a royal household. But it would just be a long loan. Very long, with any luck. She and Benjy would never be soulmates, and the cat did not like him. With a flourish she handed over Benjy's lead. 'Here: Your Majesty's royal dog.'

Playback

by Ian Rankin

It was the perfect murder.

Perfect, that is, so far as the Lothian and Borders Police were concerned. The murderer had telephoned in to confess, then had panicked and attempted to flee, only to be caught leaving the scene of the crime. End of story.

Except that now he was pleading innocence. Pleading, yelling and screaming it. And this worried Detective Inspector John Rebus, worried him all the way from his office to the four-storey tenement in Leith's trendy dockside area. The tenements here were much as they were in any working-class area of Edinburgh, except that they boasted colour-splashed roller blinds at their windows, or Chinese-style bamboo affairs. And their grimy stone façades had been power-cleaned, their doors now boasting intruder-proof intercoms.

A far cry from the greasy venetian blinds and kicked-in passageways of the tenements in Easter Road or Gorgie, or even in nearby parts of Leith itself, the parts the developers were ignoring as yet.

She had worked as a legal secretary, this much Rebus knew. She had been twenty-four years of age. Her name was Moira Bitter. Rebus smiled at that. It was a guilty smile, but at this hour of the morning any smile he could raise was something of a miracle.

He parked in front of the tenement, guided by a uniformed officer who had recognised the badly dented front bumper of Rebus's car. It was rumoured that the dent had come from knocking down too many old ladies, and who was Rebus to deny it? It was the stuff of legend, and gave him prominence in the fearful eyes of the younger recruits.

A curtain twitched in one of the ground-floor windows, and Rebus caught a glimpse of an elderly lady. Every tenement, it seemed, tarted up or not, boasted its elderly lady. Living alone, with one dog or four cats for company, she was her building's eyes and ears. As Rebus entered the hallway, a door opened and the old lady stuck out her head.

'He was going to run for it,' she whispered. 'But the bobby caught him. I saw it. Is the young lass dead? Is that it?' Her lips were pursed in keen horror.

Rebus smiled at her but said nothing. She would know soon enough. Already she seemed to know as much as he did himself. That was the trouble with living in a city the size of a town, a town with a village mentality.

He climbed the four flights of stairs slowly, listening all the while to the report of the constable who was leading him inexorably towards the corpse of Moira Bitter. They spoke in an undertone: stairwell walls had ears.

'The call came at about five a.m., sir,' explained PC MacManus. 'The caller gave his name as John MacFarlane, and said he'd just murdered his girlfriend. He sounded distressed by all accounts, and I was radioed to investigate. As I arrived, a man was running down the stairs. He seemed in a state of shock.'

'Shock?'

'Sort of disorientated, sir.'

'Did he say anything?' asked Rebus.

'Yes, sir, he told me, "Thank God you're here. Moira's dead." I then asked him to accompany me upstairs to the flat in question, called in for assistance, and the gentleman was arrested.'

Rebus nodded. MacManus was a model of efficiency, not a word out of place, the tone just right. Everything by rote, and without the interference of too much thought. He would go far as a uniformed officer, but Rebus doubted the young man would ever make CID. They had reached the fourth floor. Rebus paused for breath, then walked into the flat.

The hall's pastel colour scheme extended to the living-room and bedroom. Mute colours, subtle and warming. There was nothing subtle about the blood though. The blood was copious. Moira Bitter lay sprawled across her bed, her chest a riot of colour. She was wearing apple-green pyjamas, and her hair was silky blonde. The police pathologist was examining her head.

'She's been dead about three hours,' he informed Rebus. 'Stabbed three or four times with a small sharp instrument, which, for the sake of convenience, I'm going to term a knife. I'll examine her properly later on.'

Rebus nodded, and turned to MacManus, whose face had a sickly grey tinge to it.

'Your first time?' Rebus asked.

The constable nodded slowly.

'Never mind,' Rebus continued. 'You never get used to it anyway. Come on.'

He led the constable out of the room and back into the small hallway. 'This man we've arrested, what did you say his name was?'

'John MacFarlane, sir,' said the constable, taking deep breaths. 'He's the deceased's boyfriend apparently.'

'You said he seemed in a state of shock. Was there anything else you noticed?'

The constable frowned, thinking. 'Such as, sir?' he said at last.

'Blood,' said Rebus coolly. 'You can't stab someone in the heat of the moment without getting blood on you.'

MacManus said nothing. Definitely not CID material, and perhaps realising it for the very first time. Rebus turned from him and entered the living-room. It was almost neurotically tidy. Magazines and newspapers in their rack beside the sofa. A chrome and glass coffee table bearing nothing more than a clean ashtray and a paperback romance. It could have come straight from an Ideal Homes exhibition. No family photographs, no clutter. This was the lair of an individualist. No ties with the past, and a present ransacked wholesale from Habitat and Next. There was no evidence of a struggle. No evidence of an encounter of any kind: no glasses or coffee cups. The killer had not loitered, or else had been very tidy about his business . . .

Rebus went into the kitchen. It, too, was tidy. Cups and plates stacked for drying beside the empty sink. On the draining-board were knives, forks, teaspoons. No murder weapon. There were spots of water in the sink and on the draining-board itself, yet the cutlery and crockery were dry. Rebus found a dish-towel hanging up behind the door and felt it. It was damp. He examined it more closely. There was a small smudge on it. Perhaps gravy or chocolate. Or blood. Someone had dried something recently, but what?

He went to the cutlery drawer and opened it.

Inside, amidst the various implements was a short-bladed chopping knife with a heavy black handle. A quality knife, sharp and gleaming. The other items in the drawer were bone dry, but this chopping knife's wooden handle was damp to the touch. Rebus was in no doubt: he had found his murder weapon.

Clever of MacFarlane, though, to have cleaned and put away the knife. A cool and calm action. Moira Bitter had been dead three hours. The call to the police station had come an hour ago. What had MacFarlane done during the intervening two hours? Cleaned the flat? Washed and dried the dishes? Rebus looked in the kitchen's swing-bin, but found no other clues, no broken ornaments, nothing that might hint at a struggle. And if there had been no struggle, if the murderer had gained access to the tenement and to Moira Bitter's flat without forcing an entry . . . if all this were true, Moira had known her killer.

Rebus toured the rest of the flat, but found no other clues. Beside the telephone in the hall stood an answering machine. He played the tape, and heard Moira Bitter's voice.

'Hello, this is Moira. I'm out, I'm in the bath, or I'm otherwise engaged.' (A giggle.) 'Leave a message and I'll get back to you, unless you sound boring.'

There was only one message. Rebus listened to it, then wound back the tape and listened again.

'Hello, Moira, it's John. I got your message. I'm coming over. Hope you're not "otherwise engaged". Love you.'

John MacFarlane: Rebus didn't doubt the identity of the caller. Moira sounded fresh and fancy-free in her message. But did MacFarlane's response hint at jealousy? Perhaps she *had* been otherwise engaged when he'd arrived. He'd lost his temper, blind rage, a knife lying handily . . . Rebus had seen it before. Most victims knew their attackers. If that were not the case, the police wouldn't solve so many crimes. It was a blunt fact. You double-bolted your door against the psychopath with the chainsaw, only to be stabbed in the back by your lover, husband, son or neighbour.

John MacFarlane was as guilty as hell. They would find blood on his clothes, even if he'd tried cleaning it off. He had stabbed his girlfriend, then calmed down and called in to report the crime, but had grown frightened at the end and had attempted to flee.

The only question left in Rebus's mind was the why? The why?, and those missing two hours.

Edinburgh in the early hours. The occasional taxi rippling across cobblestones, and lone shadowy figures slouching home with hands in pockets, shoulders hunched. During the night hours, the sick and the old died peacefully, either at home or in some hospital ward. Two in the morning until four: the dead hours. And then some died horribly, with terror in their eyes. The taxis still rumbled past, the night people kept moving. Rebus let his car idle at traffic lights, missing the change to green, only coming to his senses as amber turned red again. Glasgow Rangers were coming to town on Saturday. There would be casual violence. Rebus felt comfortable with the thought. The worst football hooligan could probably not have stabbed with the same ferocity as Moira Bitter's killer. Rebus lowered his eyebrows. He was rousing himself to fury, keen for confrontation. Confrontation with the murderer himself.

John MacFarlane was crying as he was led into the interrogation room, where Rebus had made himself look comfortable, cigarette in one hand, coffee in the other. Rebus had expected a lot of things, but not tears.

'Would you like something to drink?' he asked.

MacFarlane shook his head. He had slumped into the chair on the other side of the desk, his shoulders sagging, head bowed, and the sobs still coming from his throat. He mumbled something.

'I didn't catch that,' said Rebus.

'I said I didn't do it,' MacFarlane answered quietly. 'How could I do it? I love Moira.'

Rebus noted the present tense. He gestured towards the tape machine on the desk. 'Do you have any objection to my making a recording of this interview?'

MacFarlane shook his head again.

Rebus switched on the machine. He flicked ash from his cigarette on to the floor, sipped his coffee, and waited. Eventually, MacFarlane looked up. His eyes were stinging red. Rebus stared hard into those eyes, but still said nothing. MacFarlane seemed to be calming. Seemed, too, to know what was expected of him. He asked for a cigarette, was given one, and started to speak.

'I'd been out in my car. Just driving, thinking.'

Rebus interrupted him. 'What time was this?'

'Well,' said MacFarlane, 'ever since I left work, I suppose. I'm an architect. There's a competition on just now to design a new art gallery and museum complex in Stirling. Our partnership's going in for it. We were discussing ideas most of the day, you know, brainstorming.' He looked up at Rebus again, and Rebus nodded. Brainstorm: now there was an interesting word . . .

'And after work,' MacFarlane continued, 'I was so

fired up I just felt like driving. Going over the different options and plans in my head. Working out which was strongest . . . '

He broke off, realising perhaps that he was talking in a rush, without thought or caution. He swallowed and inhaled some smoke. Rebus was studying MacFarlane's clothes. Expensive leather brogues. Brown corduroy trousers. A thick white cotton shirt, the kind cricketers wore, open at the neck. And a tailor-made tweed jacket. MacFarlane's 3-Series BMW was parked in the police garage, and being searched. His pockets had been emptied, a Liberty-print tie confiscated in case he had ideas about hanging himself. His brogues, too, were without their laces, these having been confiscated along with the tie. Rebus had gone through the belongings. A wallet, not exactly bulging with money but containing a fair spread of credit cards. There were more cards, too, in MacFarlane's personal organiser. Rebus flipped through the diary pages, then turned to the sections for notes and for addresses. MacFarlane seemed to lead a busy but quite normal life.

Rebus studied him now, across the expanse of the old table. MacFarlane was well built, handsome if you liked that sort of thing. He looked strong, but not brutish. Probably he would make the local news headlines as 'Secretary's Yuppie Killer'. Rebus stubbed out his cigarette.

'We know you did it, John. That's not in dispute. We just want to know why.'

MacFarlane's voice was brittle with emotion. 'I swear I didn't, I swear.'

'You're going to have to do better than that.' Rebus paused again. Tears were dripping on to MacFarlane's corduroys. 'Go on with your story,' he said.

MacFarlane shrugged. 'That's about it,' he said, wiping his nose with the sleeve of his shirt.

Rebus prompted him. 'You didn't stop off anywhere for petrol or a meal or anything like that?' He sounded sceptical.

MacFarlane shook his head. 'No, I just drove until my head was clear. I went all the way to the Forth Road Bridge. Turned off and went into Queensferry. Got out of the car to have a look at the water. Threw a few stones in for luck.' He smiled at the irony. 'Then drove round the coast road and back into Edinburgh.'

'Nobody saw you? You didn't speak to anyone?'

'Not that I can remember.'

'And you didn't get hungry?' Rebus sounded entirely unconvinced.

'We'd had a business lunch with a client. We took him to the Eyrie. After a lunch there, I seldom need to eat until the next morning.'

The Eyrie was Edinburgh's most expensive restaurant. You didn't go there to eat, you went there to spend money. Rebus was feeling peckish himself. The canteen did a fine bacon buttie . . .

'When did you last see Miss Bitter alive?'

At the word 'alive', MacFarlane shivered. It took him a long time to answer. Rebus watched the tape revolving. 'Yesterday morning,' MacFarlane said at last. 'She stayed the night at my flat.'

'How long have you known her?'

'About a year. But I only started going out with her a couple of months ago.'

'Oh? And how did you know her before that?'

MacFarlane paused. 'She was Kenneth's girlfriend,' he said at last.

'Kenneth being . . . ?'

MacFarlane's cheeks reddened before he spoke. 'My

best friend,' he said. 'Kenneth was my best friend. You could say I stole her from him. These things happen, don't they?'

Rebus raised an eyebrow. 'Do they?' he said.

MacFarlane bowed his head again. 'Can I have a coffee?' he asked quietly.

Rebus nodded, then lit another cigarette.

MacFarlane sipped the coffee, holding it in both hands like a shipwreck survivor. Rebus rubbed his nose and stretched, feeling tired. He checked his watch. Eight in the morning. What a life. A string of bacon rind curled across the plate in front of him. He had eaten two bacon rolls. MacFarlane had refused food, but finished the first cup of coffee in two gulps, and gratefully accepted a second.

'So,' Rebus said, 'you drove back into town.'

'That's right.' MacFarlane took another sip of coffee. 'I don't know why, but I decided to check my answering machine for calls.'

'You mean when you got home?'

MacFarlane shook his head. 'No, from the car. I called home from my car phone and got the answering machine to play back any messages.'

Rebus was impressed. 'That's clever,' he said.

MacFarlane smiled again, but the smile soon vanished. 'One of the messages was from Moira,' he said. 'She wanted to see me.'

'At that hour?' MacFarlane shrugged. 'Did she say why she wanted to see you?'

'No. She sounded . . . strange.'

'Strange?'

'A bit . . . I don't know, distant maybe.'

'Did you get the feeling she was on her own when she called?'

'I've no idea.'

'Did you call her back?'

'Yes, I think so. Her answering machine was on. I left a message.'

'Would you say you're the jealous type, Mr MacFarlane?'

'What?' MacFarlane sounded surprised by the question. He seemed to give it serious thought. 'No more so than the next man,' he said at last.

'Why would anyone want to kill her?'

MacFarlane stared at the table, shaking his head slowly.

'Go on,' said Rebus, sighing, growing impatient. 'You were saying how you got her message.'

'Well, I went straight to her flat. It was late, but I knew if she was asleep I could always let myself in.'

'Oh?' Rebus was interested. 'How?'

'She gave me a spare key,' MacFarlane explained.

Rebus got up from his chair and walked to the far wall and back, deep in thought. 'I don't suppose,' he said, 'you've got any idea *when* Moira made that call?'

MacFarlane shook his head. 'But the machine will have logged it,' he said. Rebus was more impressed than ever. Technology was a wonderful thing. What's more, he was impressed by MacFarlane. If the man was a murderer, then he was a very good one, for he had fooled Rebus into thinking him innocent. It was crazy. There was nothing to point to him *not* being guilty. But all the same, a feeling was a feeling, and Rebus most definitely had a feeling.

'I want to see that machine,' he said. 'And I want to hear the message on it. I want to hear Moira's last words.'

* * *

It was interesting how the simplest cases could become so complex. There was still no doubt in the minds of those around Rebus – his superiors and those below him – that John MacFarlane was guilty of murder. They had all the proof they needed, every last bit of it circumstantial.

MacFarlane's car was clean: no bloodstained clothes stashed in the boot. There were no prints on the chopping-knife, though MacFarlane's prints were found elsewhere in the flat – not surprising given that he'd visited that night, as well as on many a previous one. No prints either on the kitchen sink and taps, though the murderer had washed a bloody knife. Rebus thought that curious . . . And as for motive: jealousy, a falling-out, a past indiscretion discovered. The CID had seen them all.

Murder by stabbing was confirmed, and the time of death narrowed down to a quarter of an hour either side of three in the morning. At which time MacFarlane claimed he was driving towards Edinburgh, but with no witnesses to corroborate the claim. There was no blood to be found on MacFarlane's clothing, but, as Rebus himself knew, that didn't mean the man wasn't a killer.

More interesting, however, was that MacFarlane denied making the call to the police. Yet someone – in fact, whoever murdered Moira Bitter – *had* made it. And more interesting even than this was the telephone answering machine.

Rebus went to MacFarlane's flat in Liberton to investigate. The traffic was busy coming into town, but quiet heading out. Liberton was one of Edinburgh's many anonymous middle-class districts, substantial houses, small shops, a busy thoroughfare. It looked innocuous at midnight, and was even safer by day.

What MacFarlane had termed a 'flat' comprised, in fact, the top two storeys of a vast, detached house. Rebus roamed the building, not sure if he was looking for anything in particular. He found little. MacFarlane led a rigorous and regimented life, and had the home to accommodate such a lifestyle. One room had been turned into a makeshift gymnasium, with weightlifting equipment and the like. There was an office for business use, and a study for private use. The main bedroom was decidedly masculine in taste, though a framed painting of a naked woman had been removed from one wall and tucked behind a chair. Rebus thought he detected Moira Bitter's influence at work.

In the wardrobe were a few pieces of her clothing and a pair of her shoes. A snapshot of her had been framed and placed on MacFarlane's bedside table. Rebus studied the photograph for a long time. Then sighed and left the bedroom, closing the door after him. Who knew when John MacFarlane would see his home again . . .

The answering machine was in the living-room. Rebus played the tape of the previous night's calls. Moira Bitter's voice was clipped and confident, her message to the point: 'Hello.' Then a pause. 'I need to see you. Come round as soon as you get this message. Love you.'

MacFarlane had told Rebus that the display unit on the machine showed time of call. Moira's call registered at three-fifty a.m., about forty-five minutes after her death. There was room for some discrepancy, but not three-quarters of an hour's worth. Rebus scratched his chin and pondered. He played the tape again. 'Hello,' then the pause. 'I need to see you.' He stopped the tape and played it again, this time with the volume up and his ear close to the machine. That pause was curious, and the sound quality on the tape was poor. He rewound and listened to another call from the same evening. The quality was better, the voice much clearer. Then he listened to Moira again. Were these recording machines infallible? Of course not. The time display could have been tampered with. The recording itself could be a fake. After all, whose word did he have that this *was* the voice of Moira Bitter? Only John MacFarlane's. But John MacFarlane had been caught leaving the scene of a murder. And now here Rebus was being presented with a sort of an alibi for the man. Yes, the tape could well be a fake, used by MacFarlane to substantiate his story, but stupidly not put into use until after the time of death. Still, from what Rebus had heard from Moira's own answering machine, the voice was certainly similar to her own. The lab boys could sort it out with their clever machines. One technician in particular owed him a rather large favour . . .

Rebus shook his head. This still wasn't making much sense. He played the tape again and again.

'Hello.' Pause. 'I need to see you.'

'Hello.' Pause. 'I need to see you.'

'Hello.' Pause. 'I need – ' . . .

And suddenly it became a little clearer in his mind. He ejected the tape and slipped it into his jacket pocket, then picked up the telephone and called the station. He asked to speak to Detective Sergeant Brian Holmes. The voice, when it came on the line, was tired but amused.

'Don't tell me,' Holmes said, 'let me guess. You want me to drop everything and run an errand for you.'

'You must be psychic, Brian. Two errands really. Firstly, last night's calls. Get the recording of them and search for one from John MacFarlane, claiming he'd just killed his girlfriend. Make a copy of it and wait there for me. I've got another tape for you, and I want them both taken to the lab. Warn them you're coming— '

' —and tell them it's priority, I know. It's *always* priority. They'll say what they always say: give us four days.'

'Not this time,' Rebus said. 'Ask for Bill Costain and tell him Rebus is collecting on his favour. He's to shelve what he's doing. I want a result today, not next week.'

'What's the favour you're collecting on?'

'I caught him smoking dope in the lab toilets last month.'

Holmes laughed. 'The world's going to pot,' he said.

Rebus groaned at the joke and put down the receiver. He needed to speak with John MacFarlane again. Not about lovers this time, but about friends . . .

Rebus rang the doorbell a third time, and at last heard a voice from within.

'Jesus, hold on! I'm coming.'

The man who answered the door was tall, thin, wire-framed glasses perched on his nose. He peered at Rebus and ran his fingers through his hair.

'Mr Thomson?' Rebus asked. 'Kenneth Thomson?'

'Yes,' said the man, 'that's right.'

Rebus flipped open his ID. 'Detective Inspector John Rebus,' he said by way of introduction. 'May I come in?'

Kenneth Thomson held open the door. 'Please do,' he said. 'Will a cheque be all right?'

'A cheque?'

'I take it you're here about the parking tickets,' said

Thomson. 'I'd have got round to them eventually, believe me. It's just that I've been hellish busy, and what with one thing and another . . . '

'No, sir,' said Rebus, his smile as cold as a church pew, 'nothing to do with parking fines.'

'Oh?' Thomson pushed his glasses back up his nose and looked at Rebus. 'Then what's the problem?'

'It's about Miss Moira Bitter,' said Rebus.

'Moira? What about her?'

'She's dead, sir.'

Rebus had followed Thomson into a cluttered room overflowing with bundles of magazines and newspapers. A hi-fi sat in one corner, and covering the wall next to it were shelves filled with cassette tapes. These had an orderly look to them, as though they had been indexed, each tape's spine carrying an identifying number.

Thomson, who had been clearing a chair for Rebus to sit on, froze at the detective's words.

'Dead?' he gasped. 'How?'

'She was murdered, sir. We think John MacFarlane did it.'

'John?' Thomson's face was quizzical, then sceptical, then resigned. 'But why?'

'We don't know that yet, sir. I thought you might be able to help.'

'Of course I'll help if I can. Sit down, please.'

Rebus perched on the chair, while Thomson pushed aside some newspapers and settled himself on a sofa.

'You're a writer, I believe,' said Rebus.

Thomson nodded distractedly. 'Yes,' he said. 'Freelance journalism, food and drink, travel, that sort of thing. Plus the occasional commission to write a book. That's what I'm doing now, actually. Writing a book.'

'Oh? I like books myself. What's it about?'

'Don't laugh,' said Thomson, 'but it's a history of the haggis.'

'The haggis?' Rebus couldn't disguise the smile in his voice, warmer this time: the church pew had been given a cushion. He cleared his throat noisily, glancing around the room, noting the piles of books leaning precariously against walls, the files and folders and newsprint cuttings. 'You must do a lot of research,' he said appreciatively.

'Sometimes,' said Thomson. Then he shook his head. 'I still can't believe it. About Moira, I mean. About John.'

Rebus took out his notebook, more for effect than anything else. 'You were Miss Bitter's lover for a while,' he stated.

'That's right, Inspector.'

'But then she went off with Mr MacFarlane.'

'Right again.' A hint of bitterness had crept into Thomson's voice. 'I was very angry at the time, but I got over it.'

'Did you still see Miss Bitter?'

'No.'

'What about Mr MacFarlane?'

'No again. We spoke on the telephone a couple of times. It always seemed to end in a shouting match. We used to be like . . . well, it's a cliché, I suppose, but we used to be like brothers.'

'Yes,' said Rebus, 'so Mr MacFarlane told me.'

'Oh?' Thomson sounded interested. 'What else did he say?'

'Not much really.' Rebus rose from his perch and went to the window, holding aside the net curtain to stare out on to the street below. 'He said you'd known each other for years.'

'Since school,' Thomson added.

Rebus nodded. 'And he said you drove a black Ford Escort. That'll be it down there, parked across the street.'

Thomson came to the window. 'Yes,' he agreed uncertainly, 'that's it. But I don't see what— '

'I noticed it as I was parking my own car,' Rebus continued, brushing past Thomson's interruption. He let the curtain fall and turned back into the room. 'I noticed you've got a car alarm. I suppose you must get a lot of burglaries around here?'

'It's not the most salubrious part of town,' Thomson said. 'Not all writers are Jeffrey Archer.'

'Did money have anything to do with it?' Rebus asked.

Thomson paused. 'With what, Inspector?'

'With Miss Bitter leaving you for Mr MacFarlane. He's not short of a bob or two, is he?'

Thomson's voice rose perceptibly. 'Look, I really can't see what this has to do with— '

'Your car was broken into a few months ago, wasn't it?' Rebus was examining a pile of magazines on the floor now. 'I saw the report. They stole your radio and your car phone.'

'Yes.'

'I notice you've replaced the car phone.' He glanced up at Thomson, smiled, and continued browsing.

'Of course,' said Thomson. He seemed confused now, unable to fathom where the conversation was leading.

'A journalist would need a car phone, wouldn't he?' Rebus observed. 'So people could keep in touch, contact him at any time. Is that right?'

'Absolutely right, Inspector.'

Rebus threw the magazine back on to the pile and nodded slowly. 'Great things, car phones.' He walked over towards Thomson's desk. It was a small flat. This room obviously served a double purpose as study and living-room. Not that Thomson entertained many visitors. He was too aggressive for many people, too secretive for others. So John MacFarlane had said.

On the desk sat more clutter, though in some appearance of organisation. There was also a neat word processor, and beside it a telephone. And next to the telephone sat an answering machine.

'Yes,' Rebus repeated. 'You need to be in contact.' Rebus smiled towards Thomson. 'Communication, that's the secret. And I'll tell you something else about journalists.'

'What?' Unable to comprehend Rebus's direction, Thomson's tone had become that of someone bored with a conversation. He shoved his hands deep into his pockets.

'Journalists are hoarders.' Rebus made this sound like some great wisdom. His eyes took in the room again. 'I mean, near-pathological hoarders. They can't bear to throw things away, because they never know when something might become useful. Am I right?'

Thomson shrugged.

'Yes,' said Rebus, 'I bet I am. Look at these cassettes, for example.' He went to where the rows of tapes were neatly displayed. 'What are they? Interviews, that sort of thing?'

'Mostly, yes,' Thomson agreed.

'And you still keep them, even though they're years old?'

Thomson shrugged again. 'So I'm a hoarder.'

But Rebus had noticed something on the top shelf, some plain brown cardboard boxes. He reached up and lifted one down. Inside were more tapes, marked with months and years. But these tapes were smaller.

Rebus gestured with the box towards Thomson, his eyes seeking an explanation.

Thomson smiled uneasily. 'Answering machine messages,' he said.

'You keep these, too?' Rebus sounded amazed.

'Well,' Thomson said, 'someone may agree to something over the phone, an interview or something, then deny it later. I need them as records of promises made.'

Rebus nodded, understanding now. He replaced the brown box on its shelf. He still had his back to Thomson when the telephone rang, a sharp electronic sound.

'Sorry,' Thomson apologised, going to answer it.

'Not at all.'

Thomson picked up the receiver. 'Hello?' He listened, then frowned. 'Of course,' he said finally, holding the receiver out towards Rebus. 'It's for you, Inspector.'

Rebus raised a surprised eyebrow, and accepted the receiver.

'Hello?'

It was, as he had known it would be, Detective Sergeant Holmes.

'Okay,' Holmes said. 'Costain no longer owes you that favour. He's listened to both tapes. He hasn't run all the necessary tests yet, but he's pretty convinced.'

'Go on.' Rebus was looking at Thomson, who was sitting, hands clasping knees, on the arm of the chair.

'The call we received last night,' said Holmes, 'the one from John MacFarlane admitting to the murder of Moira Bitter, originated from a portable telephone.'

'Interesting,' said Rebus, his eyes on Thomson. 'And what about the other one?'

'Well, the tape you gave me seems to be twice-removed.'

'What does that mean?'

'It means,' said Holmes, 'that according to Costain it's not just a recording, it's the *recording* of a recording.'

Rebus nodded, satisfied. 'Okay, thanks, Brian.' He put down the receiver.

'Good news or bad?' Thomson asked.

'A bit of both,' answered Rebus thoughtfully.

Thomson had risen to his feet. 'I feel like a drink, Inspector. Can I get you one?'

'It's a bit early for me, I'm afraid,' Rebus said, looking at his watch. It was eleven o'clock: opening time. 'All right,' he said, 'just a small one.'

'The whisky's in the kitchen,' Thomson explained. 'I'll just be a moment.'

'Fine, sir, fine.'

Rebus listened as Thomson left the room and headed off towards the kitchen. He stood beside the desk, thinking through what he now knew. Then, hearing Thomson returning from the kitchen, floorboards bending beneath his weight, he picked up the wastepaper basket from below the desk, and, as Thomson entered the room, proceeded to empty the contents in a heap on the sofa.

Thomson stood in the doorway, a glass of whisky in each hand, dumbstruck. 'What on earth are you doing?' he spluttered at last. But Rebus ignored him and started to pick through the now strewn contents of the bin, talking as he searched.

'It was pretty close to being foolproof, Mr Thomson. Let me explain. The killer went to Moira Bitter's flat, and talked her into letting him in, despite the late hour. He murdered her quite callously, let's make no mistake about that. I've never seen so much premeditation in a case before. He cleaned the knife and returned it to its drawer. He was wearing gloves, of course, knowing

John MacFarlane's fingerprints would be all over the flat, and he cleaned the knife precisely to disguise the fact that he *had* worn gloves. MacFarlane, you see, had not.'

Thomson took a gulp from one glass, but otherwise seemed rooted to the spot. His eyes had become vacant, as though picturing Rebus's story in his mind.

'MacFarlane,' Rebus continued, still rummaging, 'was summoned to Moira's flat. The message *did* come from her. He knew her voice well enough not to be fooled by someone else's voice. The killer sat outside Moira's flat, sat waiting for MacFarlane to arrive. Then the killer made one last call, this one to the police, and in the guise of an hysterical MacFarlane. We know this last call was made on a car phone. The lab boys are very clever that way. The police are hoarders, too, you see, Mr Thomson. We make recordings of emergency calls made to us. It won't be hard to voice-print that call, and try to match it to John MacFarlane. But it won't be John MacFarlane, will it?' Rebus paused for effect. 'It'll be you.'

Thomson gave a thin smile, but his grip on the two glasses had grown less steady, and whisky was dribbling from the angled lip of one of them.

'Ah-ha.' Rebus had found what he was looking for in the contents of the bin. With a pleased-as-punch grin on his unshaven, sleepless face, he pinched forefinger and thumb together and lifted them for his own and Thomson's inspection. He was holding a tiny sliver of brown recording tape.

'You see,' he continued, 'the killer had to lure MacFarlane to the murder scene. Having killed Moira, he went to his car, as I've said. There he had his portable telephone, and a cassette recorder. He was a hoarder, and had kept all his answering machine tapes, including messages left by Moira at the height of their affair. He had found the message he needed, and had spliced it. It was this message that he played, having dialled John MacFarlane's answering machine. All he had to do after that was wait. The message MacFarlane received was, "Hello, I need to see you." There was a pause after the "hello". And that pause was where the splice was made in the tape, excising this.' Rebus looked at the sliver of tape. 'The one word "Kenneth". "Hello, Kenneth, I need to see you." It was Moira Bitter talking to you, Mr Thomson, talking to you a long time ago.'

Thomson hurled both glasses at once, so that they arrowed in towards Rebus, who ducked. The glasses collided above his head, shards raining down on him. Thomson had reached the front door, had hauled it open even before Rebus was on him, lunging, pushing the younger man forwards through the doorway and on to the tenement landing. Thomson's head hit the metal rails with a muted chime, and he let out a single moan before collapsing. Rebus shook himself free of glass, feeling one or two tiny pieces nick him as he brushed a hand across his face. He brought a hand to his nose and inhaled deeply. His father had always said whisky would put hairs on his chest. Rebus wondered if the same miracle might be effected on his temples and the crown of his head . . .

It had been the perfect murder.

Well, almost. But Kenneth Thomson had reckoned without Rebus's ability actually to believe someone innocent despite the evidence against them. The case against John MacFarlane had been overwhelming. Yet Rebus, feeling it to be wrong, had been forced to invent other scenarios, other motives and other means to the fairly chilling end. It wasn't enough that Moira had died – died at the hands of someone she knew. MacFarlane had to be implicated in her murder. The killer had been out to tag them both. But it was Moira the killer hated, hated because she had broken up a friendship as well as a heart.

Rebus stood on the steps of the police station. Thomson was in a cell somewhere below his feet, somewhere below ground level. Confessing to everything. He would go to jail, while John MacFarlane, perhaps not realising his luck, had already been freed.

The streets were busy now. Lunchtime traffic, the reliable noises of the everyday. The sun was even managing to burst from its slumber. All of which reminded Rebus that his day was over. Time, all in all he felt, for a short visit home, a shower and change of clothes, and, God and the Devil willing, some sleep . . .

Murder *Ex* Africa

by Miles Tripp

The cry of a nocturnal creature pierced the hum of myriad insects as Brownlow sat at a table in his tent writing a final report but, accustomed to the night sounds of Africa, he heard nothing. All his faculties were concentrated on making the best of a bad job, providing an explanation of why his sponsored expedition had failed to discover the fossilised remains of prehistoric man.

Bones of early apes had been recovered and now lay marked and ready for crating near the tent's entrance, but these specimens dating from at least twelve million years before the advent of any species within the genus *Homo* were not uncommon and aroused little interest outside academic circles.

Earlier that evening Brownlow had called his team together, told them that finances had run out and sponsorship was being withdrawn. The bed they had been excavating, consisting of lake sediments resting on a lava base, was exhausted. After the meeting he had retired to his tent, opened a bottle of whisky and begun writing his report. This wasn't easy. His sponsors were the directors of a multinational company more interested in publicity than palaeontology. They demanded explanations in plain English shorn of technical language and terms of art.

It was now midnight and as he sat gazing blankly ahead, trying to find acceptable words to put a gloss on failure, the tent flap burst open and a young man strode in. He was carrying a globe-like object which had been wrapped in wet tissues and plaster-of-Paris bandages. Brownlow looked in disbelief as the object was carefully placed on the table beside the whisky bottle. Then, managing to keep his voice on an even, unemotional level, he asked, 'Where did you find it?'

Before replying the young man pulled up a canvas-seated chair so that he could sit opposite Brownlow. He nodded towards the whisky bottle. 'I should have brought my own booze along so we could celebrate together.'

Brownlow went to a cabinet which stood close to a camp-bed and returned with a glass tumbler. 'Help yourself,' he said. 'Now then, where did you find it?'

The young man poured a stiff measure. 'About half a mile from the site,' he replied. 'I've been doing some extra-curricular work. In my own time. I've had damn-all sleep.'

'It looks like a complete skull.'

'It is a complete skull. The parietal portion of the cranial has an indentation which I'll bet was caused by a blow from behind. I reckon my man was murdered.' His voice quickened. 'Isn't that fascinating!'

'Fascinating?'

'Yes. You know as well as I that nearly all the early finds have evidence that the subject died violently. Lends credence to the theory of innate human aggression. Ardrey called Leakey's find "Abel", a nice piece of dramatic licence and romantic crap. But I'd guess I've beaten Leakey by at least half a million years. I shall claim my old lad is Abel, first victim of man's violence.' The young man laughed. 'Only kidding,' he said, 'I'm not really into that Genesis rubbish.'

'Hold on,' said Brownlow sharply. 'I'd like some facts. Has the skull been cleaned?'

'Certainly. All proper procedures have been observed. Dental picks. Camel hair brushes. Photographs. Two native helpers as witnesses. Poor illiterates, but honest men. The evidence will stand up.' He drained his whisky and poured another measure. 'Cheers.'

Brownlow disliked Johnson, who possessed an irritating excess of youthful arrogance and had opposed him in the selection of site. Moreover, Johnson had the unpleasant habit of mixing vulgar epithets with technical language. In a discipline which required infinite patience, care and self-restraint, Johnson was a restless if brilliant maverick who lacked proper respect for his profession. It was typical of him that he should make crude jokes about the classification of Java man as *Homo erectus erectus*. But far worse was his attitude to the native workers.

It was bad enough that he had played football with them but when in the middle of a game, to the hilarity of other players, he'd stuffed a lizard down the shorts of a native worker, Brownlow had decided to call a halt to such antics and activities. He had forbidden any more games of football and threatened with dismissal any member of the team who was involved as the instigator or victim of a practical joke.

But now Brownlow's intense dislike of the younger man was modified by the realisation that, late in the eleventh hour, failure could be transformed into success. 'Have you got any sensible ideas about dating?' he asked.

'I wouldn't dream of dating you,' replied Johnson with a laugh. 'That's for sure.'

Brownlow was unamused. 'Dating your find,' he said.

'Well, we'll obviously have to see what the boys in the anatomical lab think although they'll probably be chicken and natter about ranges of tolerance. What's the bloody point of having isotopic dating and computer multivariate analysis if you can't come up with something better than a figure plus or minus a few thousand years. But I don't care. I reckon my old lad here' – and he reached out and affectionately patted the bandaged skull – 'will be recognised as the earliest example of genus *Homo*. The history books will have to be rewritten and, into the bargain, my name put into them.'

Brownlow knew he must keep calm, maintain self-control, but his annoyance was turning into a smouldering anger and his hand trembled slightly as he poured himself another drink.

'If I was a medico,' Johnson said thoughtfully, 'my old lad would be designated *Africanus Johnsonicus*. The medicos honour their great men; our lot prefer anonymity.'

It was time to squash the young man's pretensions. Brownlow eased back in his chair and said, 'You're right about it not being named after you, but wrong about credits. The credit of the find goes to the team as a whole and to me as leader.'

Johnson, glass poised halfway to his mouth, shook his head. 'Sorry, old man, but my light isn't going to be hidden under a bushel. This is my big chance. Articles in learned journals, lecture tours, the lot.' He burped and peered at the bottle. 'Where did you get this firewater? Glenfreugh. Never heard of it.'

An oil-lamp gutted momentarily before flaring up again but in the transitory shadow the older man's face became as rigid as a carving in afromosia. 'Everything is down to the leader,' he said. 'If there's success, he's the front man. If there's failure, he carries the can.'

Johnson opened his mouth to speak but was silenced by a raised hand.

'He carries the can. There's neither praise nor blame for individual members of the team.'

Johnson tossed back his whisky and reached for his bottle. 'Oh, fine! You wouldn't listen to my advice about the site. You said there was no chance of finding anything. I used initiative and my instincts, went to where I thought I'd strike gold, and came up with the goods. And you' – he jabbed a finger at the man seated opposite – 'you think you can grab credit for my achievement.'

'Don't try my patience. You know the rules.'

Johnson leaned back in his chair and gave a loud laugh. 'Rules,' he said contemptuously. 'It hasn't anything to do with rules. It's you, hanging on to your square. Fighting off the young pretender. Don't let him horn in on your preserve. That's the philosophy of the bull elephant and every other bull. And, frankly, it's bullshit.'

Very deliberately Brownlow removed the whisky bottle from the table and placed it on the dry earth floor by his feet. 'You've had enough,' he said.

'Look, boss sahib, boss sir, boss leader, I'm of age. I decide if I've had enough. I don't need your opinion.'

Brownlow's anger flared. 'You've had enough,' he repeated. 'Now get out!' He jumped to his feet and motioned towards the tent's entrance, but in making the sudden movement he kicked over the whisky bottle.

Johnson bellowed with laughter. 'You're pissed,' he said, 'and you've got the nerve to tell me I've had enough.' He stood up. 'Okay, I'm going. But when we get back to civilisation I'm going to blow the gaff on your incompetence and how the great leader wouldn't listen to my advice. I'll screw you.' He moved towards the tent's entrance.

'Come back here,' Brownlow shouted.

Pausing in mid-stride, Johnson turned and said, 'Get lost, loser.'

Brownlow moved fast. His anger had burst through all restraints. He grabbed an unpacked ape-bone and struck with all his power just as Johnson was opening the tent flap. The blow hit the back of Johnson's head and he dropped to the ground like a felled tree.

For a moment there was absolute silence broken only by the rhythmic hum of the bush and then, after gazing unbelievingly at the bone in his hand, Brownlow hurled it away. It rebounded from the inner side of the tent and came to rest near the whisky bottle.

Brownlow went on his knees and gently turned over the inert body. He felt Johnson's wrist. There was no pulse beat. Then he went to his shaving kit to fetch a steel mirror. He held it in front of Johnson's mouth which was half-open as though he was about to say something and had been interrupted. No mist formed on the mirror's polished surface. Johnson was dead.

Brownlow staggered to his feet and went back to his chair. He sat down heavily and gazed at Johnson's neatly bandaged find. It was a bitterly ironic coincidence that the prehistoric hominid had been killed by a blow to the back of its skull. The blow might even have been delivered by an ape-bone. The old Latin adage, *Ex Africa semper aliquid novi* – Out of Africa always something new – should be updated to 'Everything has happened before in Africa.'

He reached down for the bottle, unscrewed its cap

and poured a drink. This was no time for reflections. He forced himself to concentrate. There were still some hours of darkness ahead. He could look for Johnson's site, bury the skull and bury Johnson's body with it. The remains would have to be well covered to prevent discovery by prowling hyenas.

How could he explain Johnson's disappearance to the rest of the team? Say nothing? After a while someone would express anxiety about Johnson's absence. His tent and belongings would be searched for clues as to where he might have gone but, in the end, the disappearance would be written off as an insoluble mystery. Stranger things had happened in Africa.

Could he dispose of Johnson's body and yet keep the skull, thus changing a miserable failure into a spectacular triumph? A moment's thought told him this would be impracticable. There was no way he could account for having found the skull on his own and without witnesses. No. The alternatives were plain. Either he must tell the truth, stand trial in court and probably be disgraced in the eyes of his professional colleagues, or he must dispose of both body and skull and hope that when a search was made no one would discover them.

First he would have to find the spot where Johnson had made his dig. There was no time to waste. Taking a torch from the cabinet, and picking up his gun, he left the tent and went into the night.

As he walked past an acacia tree which in limpid moonlight was silhouetted like a ragged umbrella against an undulating skyline he realised he would have to deal with the two native diggers who had helped Johnson. He could guess who these men were. Johnson had been unduly friendly with some of the natives who seemed to enjoy his childish practical jokes and game-playing.

He would seek out these men, pay them off liberally, and tell them to return without delay to their homes. He would say that anything Mr Johnson had found had turned out to be valueless. Mr Johnson had accepted this verdict and retired to his tent.

He quickened his pace. The beauty of this story was that when the inevitable enquiry into Johnson's disappearance was made he could say that Johnson had been very disturbed when he realised that the find had little significance and had gone to his tent in an extremely depressed state. Perhaps depression had unhinged his mind and he had gone for a walk without taking his gun. He could – dreadful though the thought was – have been attacked by a hunting animal, dragged away to a lair and been eaten.

It wasn't difficult to locate Johnson's dig. Brownlow returned to his tent for a spade and a sheet of tarpaulin which he dowsed in disinfectant to deter any predators.

Three hours later, when a deep grave had been dug, he hauled the dead body and a piece of bloodstained canvas to the site. It was nearly daybreak when, with every limb aching from sustained effort, he finally returned to his tent. It was then he noticed the bone with which he had killed Johnson. It was the femur of an early ape of genus *Dryopithecus* and traces of blood were on the neck of the bone. Wearily he went out into the pallid half-light of daybreak and when he reached the acacia tree he threw the bone. It landed in the middle of a small bush and sank out of sight. Brownlow then went to look for the man who had assisted Johnson.

They were dispatched to their faraway homes after having been instructed that nothing found by Mr Johnson had proved to be of any value.

The team cook prepared him a breakfast of fried eggs, toast and marmalade, and a jug of steaming coffee made from beans which had been grown less than two hundred miles away. Although he was dog-tired Brownlow completed his report. His final sentences read:

> Although my valued colleague, Derek Johnson, with my permission worked an alternative site, he could find nothing better than an ape skull. However, I would like to pay tribute to his dedication and express the hope that on some future venture I shall have the pleasure of working with him.

Brownlow's plan succeeded. His story and theory about Johnson's disappearance were accepted. It was sheer bad luck that three years later a team of palaeontologists from Belgium happened to dig near the site where Johnson's body was buried and came across decomposed human remains. They also found a round object encased in plaster of Paris and perished bandages which they broke open. To their amazement they found that the object so carefully preserved was nothing more than an old football.